SPECIAL MESSAGE TO READERS

This book is published by
THE ULVERSCROFT FOUNDATION
a registered charity in the U.K., No. 264873

The Foundation was established in 1974 to provide funds to help towards research, diagnosis and treatment of eye diseases. Below are a few examples of contributions made by THE ULVERSCROFT FOUNDATION:

A new Children's Assessment Unit
at Moorfield's Hospital, London.

•

Twin operating theatres at the
Western Ophthalmic Hospital, London.

•

The Frederick Thorpe Ulverscroft Chair of
Ophthalmology at the University of Leicester.

•

Eye Laser equipment to various eye hospitals.

If you would like to help further the work of the Foundation by making a donation or leaving a legacy, every contribution, no matter how small, is received with gratitude. Please write for details to:

**THE ULVERSCROFT FOUNDATION,
The Green, Bradgate Road, Anstey,
Leicester LE7 7FU. England
Telephone: (0533)364325**

THE COURAGEOUS BREED

Colorado was a half-breed, suffering the scorn of the Apaches and the whites. When he killed in self-defence he knew his life would never be the same, and leaving the safety of his parents' ranch he rode the land alone. When he was tested he was not found wanting, and many had reason to be grateful that Colorado had in him the stuff of legend, which elevated him to that select company — The Courageous Breed.

*Books by Peter Taylor
in the Linford Western Library:*

VENGEANCE IN HIS GUNS

PETER TAYLOR

THE COURAGEOUS BREED

Complete and Unabridged

LINFORD
Leicester

First published in Great Britain in 1987 by
Robert Hale Limited
London

First Linford Edition
published November 1992
by arrangement with
Robert Hale Limited
London

Copyright © 1987 by Peter Taylor
All rights reserved

British Library CIP Data

Taylor, Peter
 The courageous breed.—Large print ed.—
Linford western library
I. Title II. Series
813.54 [F]

ISBN 0–7089–7260–8

Published by
F. A. Thorpe (Publishing) Ltd.
Anstey, Leicestershire

Set by Words & Graphics Ltd.
Anstey, Leicestershire
Printed and bound in Great Britain by
T. J. Press (Padstow) Ltd., Padstow, Cornwall

1

COLORADO leaned on the gatepost of the corral and admired the latest bunch of mustangs. Thinking of the bumps and bruises which were still to come before they could be called properly broken in, he smiled ruefully.

In some ways he preferred them wild. For him there was a certain pathos in these wild creatures bent to man's will, instead of running free in the deserts and mountains. Yet, at the same time, he was grateful. Busting broncs gave him work and it wasn't easy for a half-breed to find any in a white man's world. That was a fact.

Colorado's mother, busily preparing a pie so that it would be ready for her husband's return from Tuscon, looked out of the cabin window at her son. How tall he had grown.

She recalled vividly the years when he was but a small papoose, carried on her back as she trailed in the wake of her husband's dust across Arizona and New Mexico, evading the bluecoat soldiers. She remembered how difficult that life had been, hard enough for an Apache squaw, but for her, a white captive woman forced into marriage with an Apache warrior and unused to their ways, it had been backbreaking. Now, however, that was all memory. When her Apache husband had died, Brannigan had offered to buy her and she had wanted to go, knowing he was a good man, kind to Apaches and whites alike. Colorado left with them, sensing his mother would never go with Brannigan if it meant leaving him behind. He did not want his mother to become an old work-worn hag like so many. She realised the sacrifice he was making and now it hurt her sometimes to see the restlessness in him, the yearning for the old life. Though he never spoke of it, she knew the change had been hard for him. For twenty-three years he had lived the life of a Mimbreno Apache, nephew to the great Magnas Colorado. How hard it must have been for him to give up that kind of life, the pride of his lineage and the freedom of the south-west, in order to settle in the white man's world, but he never worried her about it, never mentioned it.

"You've taken your height as well as your name from your Uncle Magnas Colorado," she said when he came in carrying some wood. "He was six-feet-six you know."

Colorado looked in the mirror hanging on the wall and studied his high cheekbones and brown skin.

"I'm 'pache all right," he replied eventually. "There's no mistaking." But he spoke the words without bitterness, without any emotion. Only his mother felt regret. She wished he could have had enough of the white man's looks to pass easily in their world so that they could not detect his breed. But Apache was written in his every feature. She sighed fearing the trouble those features could bring him and turned back to her baking, giving herself something to do to escape worrying thoughts.

Colorado, aware of her melancholia, went over to her and wrapped an arm comfortably round her shoulder.

"You're happy ain't you, ma?" he enquired. "For sure you're happy."

She turned to him and looked up into his brown eyes and read his concern.

"How could I not be," she replied, turning away to hide her emotions from him. "I have a fine husband and a fine son." She paused and went on: "It's just that sometimes I worry about you." As she said it she was thinking of previous times she'd seen that look in his eyes, the times when he'd tried to comfort her against the abuse of children his own age who had said contemptuous words to her because of her white skin. Many battles he had fought for her when he was a child; so un-Apache-like to protect a squaw from scorn. But maybe, she reflected, some of his differences had been her fault. Perhaps she had talked too much of her own father and mother, of the security and love they'd given her, of their morals, so that he had become too sensitive for an Apache warrior. Under the cool Indian exterior he had too many conflicting emotions mirroring the confusion of his caste.

2

SUDDENLY, as she was thinking these things, she felt the big arm stiffen and when she turned to look at him again he was staring staight ahead. She followed his gaze out of the window and across the desert. The only movement she could see was some mesquite drifting as a light wind disturbed it.

"What is it, son?" she asked. What do you see?"

"Riders coming, ma — two of 'em, about an hour off."

She relaxed and he removed his arm from her shoulders. "Colorado. They can have some of my pie if it's cooked on time."

"Sure, ma, sure," he replied, unconvinced, wondering how she, who had seen so much bloodshed in her time, could trust the two strangers who were heading their way.

"You mustn't worry, son. For us the old dangerous days are done. We're settled." She smiled at him, trying to reassure him but also, unwittingly, herself.

"You forget too easily, ma," he stated blandly. "Remember how those miners whipped Magnas when he rode into their camp intending no harm. I saw the scars on his back."

She said nothing in reply. Thinking of those things only brought her pain. She and Brannigan were happy now. He was a good man, who would lay down his life for her, and for her son. In time, Colorado too might find happiness here. After all, it had only been two years since they had left the Mimbreno.

"Brannigan's due home soon," she announced, changing the subject. But her words were wasted for Colorado was already on his way out of the door as she spoke. So silently had he gone that she still thought he was at her side.

When she looked out of the window again she saw him leaning against the corral watching the small dust-cloud and there was a new tenseness in his body.

An hour later, it was as Colorado had said it would be: two riders were coming in on worn-out, dust-covered horses. When they were a mile off Colorado had known from the gait of the horses that the animals were pushed too hard, ridden carelessly. The men riding them, he calculated, were either running from something or recklessly hurrying somewhere. He figured he'd find out soon enough.

The riders pulled in near the cabin and dismounted. They didn't see Colorado as he scrutinized them. He saw that one of them was a youth about twenty years old and the other man nearer thirty. The young one, who was dressed too flashily for the desert, took a bottle from his saddle pack, took a slug, and passed it to his companion who declined the offer. Then, as he put the bottle away, he was suddenly aware of Colorado watching him. His hand moved quickly towards his Peacemaker, grabbed the butt and then froze for he saw that Colorado was unarmed and standing motionless. Relaxing, he said something to the older, darker man who turned to look. Colorado watched them, his face impassive, his back to the corral, not moving a muscle and holding their gaze. But they, as so many had done and were still to do, mistook his silence and immobility for stupidity. The pale one made a remark and the dark one laughed, only it was more of a sneering laugh than an amused one and Colorado knew there was probably going to be trouble.

The pale-skinned one strutted over to him followed by the older man, who somehow, in spite of his maturer years, seemed to be in some way subservient to the youth, a follower. They stood a couple of yards away from Colorado who still had not moved. Even his eyes did not flicker though they were seeing every movement, taking everything in.

"Need some horses, injun," the younger one said. "You got any here?"

Colorado turned round and nodded at the mustangs. "Only them," he said, lying, "But they ain't half-way broke yet." He didn't trust these two and wasn't about to mention his own horse in the barn.

"Damn it, Joe," the pale-skinned one exclaimed as he stubbed his toe petulantly into the dust. "We ain't gonna make it back in time for pa's birthday party. He'll be madder than hell."

"Horses need the rest, Billy," the older man replied mildly.

"Pesky injun's useless," the young one said, reiterating his anger, directing his spleen against the nearest person.

"You sure you ain't got no horses, injun?" Joe asked again.

"My pa has 'em," he replied. "Took 'em into town with him." He was controlling his anger, taking their insults, but hoping they would ride out quickly.

"Your pa's a damn injun too, eh?" the younger man asked malevolently, compelled by his frustration to hit out at somebody. Still Colorado kept his patience, knowing the pale-skin was all fired up with nowhere to go.

"He ain't my real pa," he said levelly and saw the pale-skin arrogantly cock an eyebrow and make assumptions.

"Hear that, Joe? White man who lives here got himself a squaw and a squaw boy too. Is the squaw woman in, boy?"

Colorado felt himself grow hotter at the calculated insults but, for his mother's sake, he sat on his temper.

"My mother's in the house," he said. "You can water the horses and rest up." Reluctantly he nodded towards the water trough, wondering at his own self-control.

The pale-skin looked at the trough and back at Colorado.

"Think we'll just go and have a

word with the squaw," he said, his eyes shifting to his partner who grinned broadly. "You wouldn't object would you, big feller?"

Colorado turned his back on them in reply. If he faced the young one he knew he could kill him with his bare hands. He left their error concerning his mother's caste uncorrected; they would find out. He heard them sniggering as they walked over to the cabin and, as soon as the door slammed, he moved quickly to the window and squatted down so that he could hear everything.

3

EVIDENTLY his mother had already welcomed them and their initial surprise had probably gone, for the first words he heard her say were, "You'll have some pie, boys. Just baked it."

"Yes, ma'am, we'd love some," a voice Colorado identified as the older man's, agreed. "We got time ain't we, Billy, while the horses rest?"

"Suppose we have. Ain't got no choice, have we," the young one grumbled sulkily.

The clink of forks striking tin plates was all Colorado heard for a few minutes. His mother, usually a chatterbox when new faces arrived, had gone quiet and he figured she'd taken their measure, as he had, and would not overdo her welcoming. He wondered how long the peace and silence would last when the pale-skinned one was around but he didn't have to wait too long to find out.

"That injun boy out there," he heard him say patronizingly, "he your son?" The question was a delicate one, which a man of true breeding would have avoided until he knew the woman better. An ignorant man, or a man lacking in tact, might have asked it in error. But Colorado knew from the youth's intonation, as he knew from his own assessment of his character, that the question was barbed, intended to hurt. An old anger roared in his belly and he knew he couldn't contain it long.

He willed his mother to deny he was her son to save herself from the youth's self-righteous gloating. But he knew she would never do that.

"Yes, and I'm mighty proud of him too," he heard her say, iron in her voice, combating the slight which rode beneath the question.

She silenced him and quiet reigned

again except for the clink of cutlery. But this youth would not give up.

"Hear tell most white women captured by 'pache kill themselves. You hear that, Joe?"

"Sure, Billy, sure." There was little interest in the older man's voice, merely complacent agreement, the easy way. But the young one whined on. "How come, ma'am, you didn't do that? Seems a likely thing to do. Those 'paches can be something terrible, uh?"

"Some Apache are bad, some are good, mister, just like whites," his mother's voice instantly came back. "And I chose life as I would every time. So would you, mister."

Colorado came to his feet as his mother spoke, the roaring anger spiralling upwards out of his belly and into his mouth, where he caught it and held it on tight lips. He felt trouble precipitating now as surely as he always knew a sandstorm was brewing before the dust clouds formed. The air was heavy with trouble.

"That son of yours, ma'am, he won't ever be acceptable in decent white homes you know," the voice droned on. "Best put him on the reservation if'n you ask me."

That did it. The anger burst through Colorado's lips in a wild Apache yell as he kicked the door open. He stood there filling the doorway, his flared nostrils announcing his anger, and his big fists bunched at his sides. It was like looking at death walking and Joe dropped his fork.

Minutes ago Colorado had seemed a docile reservation-tamed Apache, but now he was transformed. He reminded the older man of an angry brown bear which had once chased him when he was hunting in the high country. His experience told him to take the heat out of the situation so he pushed his pie away and said, "Time we looked at the horses ain't it, Billy? Wipe 'em down a bit, eh? We've a long ways to go yet."

But Billy, recovered from the shock

of Colorado's dramatic entrance, and seeing that the half-breed had still no weapon in evidence, sneered.

"No Apache bastard scares me into hurrying, Joe. That'll be the day."

"You go now, mister, and you go quick," Colorado hurled the words like a war lance into the space between them.

His mother, who had been standing at the sink trembling, fearing for her son, stepped between the men.

"Leave it, son," she said. "They'll go soon." But Colorado looked through her with hard, determined eyes and stepped aside so that he could watch Billy.

"These white trash insult us, ma, in our own house. They're as sure as hell going," he re-emphasised.

Billy looked at the Winchester just above the door and then looked at Joe, his sidekick. "Seems to me," he stated, his confidence sky high, "an Apache who ain't wearing a gun can make heap big mistake."

Then he made his mistake. With a laziness born of his confidence that Colorado carried no gun, he reached for his Peacemaker, but it was only half-way clear of the holster when Colorado pulled his knife from the top of his boot and, in one upward sweeping motion of his arm, launched it. The six-inch blade cut its way cleanly through Billy's chest and found its rest. The youth stared at it open-mouthed, disbelievingly, and then as the crimson stain grew and confirmed its ghastly reality, he stared at his companion, his eyes bulging with fear. "I'm done for, Joe," were his last words before his head and upper body hit the table.

The thumping noise broke the spell which the sight of life ebbing away had woven round his companion, and out of fear for himself Joe began to reach automatically for his 44. But half-way there, his eyes came up and met Colorado's whose Winchester was already levelled at him.

"No moves," Colorado snapped, his venom still evident. Then he turned to his mother who had slumped lifelessly into a chair. Her eyes were staring fixedly ahead, like a prophet's looking into the future seeing doom. Colorado shook her gently, his anger abating.

"They'll hang you, Colorado," she sobbed, seeing the fabrications of her dreams falling apart to be replaced by a grim vision of the future which she'd always felt was just round the corner for her son. Now it had substance.

"They won't hang me, ma. He went for his gun first." He said it to reassure her, for something to say, but he didn't believe it. But she was no longer deluded. His knife in the body, his Apache blood, were her realities now. Dreams were over.

"You'll never get a fair trial. They'll hang you before you get to court." The tears ran down her cheeks as she spoke.

"You made one hell of a mistake, kid," Joe added, finding his tongue. "That's Tom Gordon's son. He's the biggest rancher in the territory. He'll have every gunman in the territory after you within the week."

"If you live to tell it," Colorado grimaced and fear sprang into Joe's eyes as the Winchester came up again.

"Colorado!" his mother screeched, fearing her son's intentions.

"Don't worry, ma, one's enough for today. You'd better go, mister," he said flatly, "and take that excuse for a man with you."

"Sure, kid, sure, I'll go," Joe replied, relief in his voice and holding his hands up to show Colorado he had no intention of drawing. "I ain't gonna go up against you. No need. You're a dead man anyhow."

Joe shouldered the body and, while Colorado covered him, carried it out of the cabin. Once outside, he threw it over the back of one horse and led both horses to the trough where he let them drink. Then he mounted the free horse and kicked it into a canter, leading the other behind.

4

COLORADO and his mother watched him go. It was half in Colorado's mind to shoot him while he was still in range. He knew that's what an Apache would have done and cursed the part of his mother in himself which wouldn't let him do it. The man was a follower with no mind of his own, but he had done no real harm. He turned away knowing his restraint could cost him a heap of trouble.

"You'll have to go back," his mother said in a monotone, and sat down on the bench outside the cabin.

"Back? Back where, ma?"

"Back to the Mimbrenos," she said in a whisper, the effort she was making to control her emotions etching lines round her mouth so that she looked much older. Her mind was searching, trying to be practical for her son's sake.

"He drew first, ma," Colorado said softly again.

"He ain't going to say that, is he?" She pointed to the man and horses moving across the chaparral. "I've heard of this Tom Gordon. He's a powerful man and that feller will be too scared to tell him that he allowed his son to get into a mess of trouble. He'll look after his own hide that one."

Colorado nodded his understanding. "Back to the Mimbreno, uh!"

"It was bound to come to that anyway," she said fatalistically. "I was a fool to leave, thinking of myself instead of you. Folk ain't nowhere near ready to accept anything Apache." She let out a long sigh. "I'll come with you. Brannigan will too."

She tried to get up but she was shaking, her limbs weak from shock. Colorado put a restraining arm on her shoulder.

"That life's too hard for you now,

ma," he said. "Ain't you happy here with Brannigan? You've got to be fair to him too. That ain't no way for him either, not now."

"We'd manage," she started to say, "I . . . " But he had gently pressed his fingers to her lips, silencing her.

"It's time I struck out on my own. Know'd it a long time now."

She looked up at him towering over her and knew it was true. Time had ridden over her and she was not hardy enough to live the Apache way. Physically, time had not marked her son. The yearning for the trail, for the unpredictable, was in him as it was in most youths, but in one with Apache blood who had known their ways it was compelling.

"I'll get your things," she said, rising, conceding he was correct and acting against all motherly instincts because she knew it was the right and practical thing to do for the sake of saving his life.

Colorado went to the barn and

saddled the horse he hadn't mentioned to the two drifters. Then he went into the cabin and prepared his weapons while his mother packed some clothes and food into his warbag.

He took the Winchester knowing that Brannigan wouldn't mind. It was a good rifle and he was used to it.

In the bedroom he took out the gun-belt Brannigan had given him, strapped it to his waist and slid the Colt into the holster. The knife which he had retrieved from Billy Gordon's body was slipped into his boot. Finally, he adjusted the gunbelt until he wore it high as Brannigan had shown him.

"How'll I find 'em, ma," he said when his mother came into the bedroom.

"Go to San Carlos Reservation and find Lobo. He will know. There ain't many they trust but they trust him."

He pulled on the knee-length moccasins and tied the Winchester diagonally across his shoulders. His mother watched him and when he'd finished she gave him his war-bag.

Without speaking they went out to the waiting horse.

Before he mounted he looked at his mother, bent over and kissed her forehead. Their eyes met and Colorado knew the things he was remembering about her would go with him now, sometimes to warm him, sometimes to haunt him. For mother and son the past and present were encapsulated into that moment which was lost as soon as Colorado turned and climbed into the saddle.

"Take care, ma," he said softly and kicked the horse into action, heading it out to the desert country which he understood so well. He looked back once to wave to her and set his mind ahead.

5

TWO days later, in the early morning, Colorado rode into the San Carlos Reservation. As he rode through the camp he detected the difference between it and the camps he had lived in and it disturbed him. Outside one jacale four men were squatting drinking mescale and hearing them talk Colorado knew they were half-way to being drunk. In another part of the camp other Apache men and women were digging irrigation ditches and that too he found strange. The Apache he had lived with always abhorred the idea of becoming farmers, being traditionally hunters and warriors.

He rode right into the camp, dismounted and walked his horse, wondering in which of the wickiups he would find Lobo.

"Who do you seek?" a voice behind him asked and he turned to see the questioner was an old squaw.

"I come seeking Lobo. He was once chief of the Mimbreno."

"Once is a good word here, tall one. His wickiup up there," she said, pointing. "But do not stay too long here for you will surely become a half man if you do."

"I will remember your words," he replied, "for I remember the day when the Apache could not think any man was more powerful than he."

He heard the old woman cackling as he walked the horse to Lobo's wickiup and called the old chief. Eventually the flap went back and an old man, stiff with age, emerged, shielding his eyes against the sudden light as he tried to focus on the man who had used his name.

A minute passed as they studied each other. Colorado read strength in the old man's features and remembered how once he had been venerated amongst the Mimbreno.

"It is you," Lobo said finally in a strong voice which belied the stiffness of age which had been evident in his limbs.

"My mother sent me to you," Colorado said, respect in his voice. "I need to go back to Magnas."

The old Apache raised his eyebrows. "First we talk and smoke, eh?" and gestured at the inside of the wickiup.

When they were seated, the old man lit a pipe and in silence they took turns to smoke it. Then the old man came to the point.

"Why do you wish to find Magnas?"

Colorado told him the story of how he had come to kill Billy Gordon.

"It's an old story," the chief said when Colorado had finished. "Your mother was right to send you. The White Man has no justice for the Apache." He blew smoke into the air and as he watched it curl away he said, "Magnas is at White Springs. You remember it, uh?"

Colorado nodded. It was a camp

they'd often used when he'd been with them and he remembered how to find it.

The old one looked straight at him. "It will be hard for you. Always there will be someone to reject your white blood. You know this. It will be their excuse, when things go wrong, to turn on you."

"I know it."

"A man who lives in two camps," Lobo went on, re-emphasising his point, "is sometimes ambushed as he rides between them. In this country a man must keep one camp."

Colorado took a puff on the pipe and passed it back to Lobo. "Your words, as ever, are wise and will be remembered."

They talked for a while after that. Lobo told him of the troubles on the Reservation; how the white contractors supplied them with sick cows for meat; how they were kept short of blankets; how the young ones were bored and drinking. The picture he painted was a depressing one.

When it was time to go they embraced outside the wickiup and wished each other good luck. As he headed out for White Springs, Colorado hoped Lobo's welcome would be matched by the Mimbrenos'.

Two days riding saw Colorado arrive in the vicinity of White Springs Camp. Two needle rocks, visible miles away, guarded a long canyon which opened eventually into a basin-shaped hollow where there were two seeps which provided plentiful water most of the year. Anyone riding up to it in daylight could be seen in the far distance by sentries positioned on the tall rocks and Colorado knew that certainly he'd already been seen by sharp, desert eyes.

But he didn't want to ride too close, to show much interest in White Springs during daylight. So he took it easy judging his pace and then, in the early twilight, pitched his camp in the foothills. Instead of using the easily combustible curl leaf which abounded and which would be almost smokeless, he found some ironwood trees and built his fire from their branches knowing it would burn bright this way and that the Apaches would feel safe knowing that the stranger had settled for the night. They would not come for him in the dark. They would figure that there was no way he could go now to evade them. They would wait for the morrow.

But his plan pre-empted them. In the middle of the night he rose, built the fire up and moved out between the needle rocks and into the canyon. When he was a half mile in he halted, tethered his horse near some galleto grass and worked his way back on foot to one of the needle rocks.

It took him an hour to find the mustang. He knew that the sentry would leave it tethered somewhere near the base of the rock but, in the darkness, it had not been easy to find. Gently, coaxing it with easy words, he led the animal away and back to his own horse.

When morning light came, it found him further up the canyon, almost on top of the Apache camp. He saw small wisps of smoke from the cooking fires and then the wickiups themselves. Slowly, he rode in, trailing the sentry's horse behind him. Some of the men, just rising, came out of their wickiups and stared at him. Here and there he could hear an Apache guffaw as he realised the significance of the spare horse Colorado was pulling behind him. That was why he had done it. First impressions were important with an Apache and they rated trickery and guile above any foolhardy bravery. Taking the horse from the sentry would amuse and perhaps make his re-acceptance easier and more light-hearted.

Some of the watching Apaches recognised him whilst others could see he was Apache bred and did not fear his presence. So he rode unimpeded through the camp. He asked one of the squaws which was the wickiup of the chief and she gestured at a large one in the centre of the camp. Colorado dismounted, led the horse behind him and stood outside the wickiup waiting.

He had waited twenty minutes before the chiefs huge form emerged. Magnas stretched his well-muscled, large body to the sun and did not see Colorado for a second. Then the eyes alighted on him and penetrated, wondering. In that one look, before recognition, Colorado saw the wariness and strength that marked the chief of the Mimbreno. Recognition softened the look and Magnas came forward, his huge arms stretched out to embrace his nephew.

"Greetings, uncle," Colorado said, meeting his uncle's embrace and feeling the strength in the body of the chief. "Even at sixty years, you're as strong as a young man," he added as they unlocked.

"You have come back to us,

Colorado," Magnas stated, his voice clear. "Your mother is well?"

"She is well, uncle, and sends you greetings."

Magnas nodded. "It is good that she is well and you return. It will be a long stay, I hope?"

"The gods of the mountain and you yourself will decide that, uncle. There was trouble with the whites. I killed a man and have had to run from them."

"This was sure to happen." Magnas's voice was edged with cynicism born of bitter experience. Colorado recalled that the chiefs wife and child had been murdered by white men many years ago and how he'd never got over it.

"You will eat breakfast with me," Magnas announced and then seeing the two horses and recognising one as an Indian pony, his eyes twinkled. "You have remembered our ways, Colorado."

One of the Apache led the horses away to be fed and watered and the two of them sat down to a breakfast of mule meat. Colorado enjoyed the meal and as he ate an old friend came up to greet him so that he began to feel at home and that his decision to return was the right one.

But just as he had finished his meal, he sensed someone approaching a little too quickly, and half turned. When he recognised the Apache and saw the ill-humour on his face, he sprang to his feet and faced him, standing wide-legged, prepared for an onslaught if it came. Magnas, however, remained sitting, watching calmly, retaining his quiet dignity.

"So it is you who took my mustang," Snake Eye said, taking his stance a yard away, his eyes bulging with hatred.

Colorado held their glare and inwardly cursed his luck. Snake Eye just would have to be the one who was on guard. Another Mimbreno would have come into the camp perturbed but then would have seen the joke. But with this one there was an old hatred. His wife, Raven Wing, had favoured

Colorado when they were young. Snake Eye had known this and always had been consumed by jealousy. The other Apaches were watching now, wondering where the confrontation would lead.

Colorado saw Raven Wing emerge from a wickiup and join the others. Snake Eye saw her too and his shoulders stiffened. Colorado spotted this and knew the mustang had become a thing of immense pride instead of a light-hearted affair.

Nevertheless he was newly arrived. He didn't want trouble and he tried appeasement choosing his words carefully.

"It was a foolish prank, Snake Eye. I am sorry. You must forgive me trying to show off, eh?"

The words were conciliatory, not a warrior's, and few of the Apaches there would have spoken them. But Snake Eye's anger, and a blinding cloud in his memory, did not allow him to see this.

He spat at the ground near Colorado's

feet. "Why do you return, White Eyes? Do you spy on us and carry tales back to the fort, uh?"

Mutterings amongst the crowd told Colorado that the question was one that would need answering. Some of them were evidently wary of him. Lobo had warned him well. Already one of the Mimbrenos was challenging his blood. He was about to reply when Magnas, who had been listening without interfering, chipped in.

"Colorado is of my blood, Snake Eye. Accuse him and you accuse me.

"Part of him is of your blood, Magnas," Snake Eye came back. "Part of his blood is that of the White Eyes. This is the part of him I challenge."

The answer had been snappy and surprised Colorado who could remember a time when nobody would have spoken back to the chief. But Magnas was older now and perhaps some of the young bloods were feeling their way. Snake Eye apparently was and the murmurs of approval his reasoning brought from the crowd, confirmed it.

Encouraged by their support, Snake Eye got the bit between his teeth. "There is a simple test, Magnas, if he is not afraid."

Magnas looked at them both, wanting to protect Colorado but knowing that the voice of his people had spoken and to go against them would not be good chieftainship. His age had mellowed him from the raw, violent leader Colorado had known, to the diplomatic stateman.

Colorado was anxious to avoid forcing his uncle to make the decision.

"I'll do what you wish," he said, but uncomfortably seeing that Snake Eye seemed pretty sure of himself.

When they looked at him, Magnas nodded his consent.

6

SNAKE EYE triumphantly jerked his head at Colorado indicating he should follow him. They moved off together with the curious crowd following behind them. Snake Eye halted a little way clear of the wickiups and smiled evilly at Colorado, showing a mouthful of black teeth.

"There is your test," he announced, pointing, and Colorado saw the three white men tied to stakes about twenty yards ahead. His mind figured what might happen and apprehension knifed through his stomach. The men were soldiers. Though they were stripped to the waist, the yellow stripes running down the sides of their trousers told him that. One of them was just a boy around nineteen years old, Colorado guessed.

Snake Eye whispered something to

someone in the crowd and he ran off but, seconds later, he was back and handed Snake Eye a bow and a quiver full of arrows. The Apache received them eagerly and draping the quiver over his shoulder he selected an arrow and fitted it to the bow. Again he looked at Colorado and showed him his teeth.

Then wordlessly he drew the bow up to his chest, withdrew the twine until it was taut, and aimed. The twang of the released string reverberated as the arrow sped towards the target. It found its home in the shoulder of one of the older soldiers and the crowd laughed. Snake Eye fitted another arrow and repeated the process putting an arrow in the soldier's other shoulder. Again and again he repeated his performance and each time, to the crowd's delight, he skilfully avoided hitting the vital organs. Colorado watched this, showing no emotion at all but growing more and more sickened as each arrow pin-cushioned the man. He felt a respect too for the man for as yet he had not screamed. But when the tenth arrow entered his body, the pent-up scream found release. The crowd's laughter rose to a crescendo as the soldier, demented now, sobbed his pain.

Snake Eye handed the bow to Colorado. "Take it Colorado," he said. "You were always good with the bow. Let your people see you kill their enemies slowly as I have done. The young one first, uh?"

Colorado looked at Magnas hoping he might veto the test, but deep down he knew the chief could do nothing. To do so, whatever he thought, would have lost him respect among his people.

Reluctantly he took the bow from Snake Eye, fitted an arrow and levelled it. As he aimed a hush fell on the crowd. Beads of sweat hung on his forehead as the sun rose higher and beat down. The young soldier's face, ash-white and portraying his fear, loomed larger than life-size to

Colorado as he drew back the bow string. Then at the final moment, he thought of his mother, her care for him when he was a boy and later a man. His fingers twitched nervously on the string. He thought of her gentleness and his disapproval of these barbarous acts and his fingers froze. The grave hand of conscience had clenched them.

Slowly and deliberately he shifted his aim to the older soldier who was whimpering like a distressed dog. He let the arrow go and it sliced cleanly into the man's heart. The whimpering ceased. The crowd was silent. The only sound was the rustling of some cottonwood trees behind them.

Snake Eye snatched the bow from Colorado like a spoiled child reclaiming its toy.

"He is white, Magnas," he sneered. "We have seen for ourselves."

The crowd of Apaches remained silent. Colorado stood still, studying their faces, and read in them their doubts about him. Lobo's words, "A man cannot keep two camps," sounded in his head. Any one of those watching, even the squaws, could have tortured the soldiers without a conscience. His uncle Magnas had done it. Several times Colorado had seen him. But he couldn't. He could kill in a fight and he could ambush because that was part of war, but he couldn't kill a defenceless man. He had often wondered how he would react if ever he was faced with such a decision. Now he knew. His mother had given him part of a white man's code which betrayed his Apache temperament. Though he loved the people his way of thinking was different.

His eyes met Snake Eye and his anger flared.

"I have not the heart of the antelope to run from my enemy," he announced to Magnas, loud enough so the crowd could hear him too. "I claim the blood rite."

A murmur rose amongst the crowd.

Magnas studied them both. "It is your right, Colorado. Does Snake Eye agree?"

Snake Eye nodded once, indicating his acceptance, and one of the more eager of the Apaches stepped out from the onlookers. With the heel of his moccasin he drew a circle, about fifteen feet in diameter, in the dust. Two other Apaches stepped forward, took out their knives and threw them into the centre of the circle. Snake Eye and Colorado faced each other across the circle of death.

Colorado took off his shirt and let it fall in the dust. There were murmurs of approval from the watchers. His torso had developed since he'd left the Mimbreno and his physique now almost matched that of the already legendary Magnas. At six feet two inches he was just an inch or two shorter than his uncle.

The spectators warmed to the prospective fight. Snake Eye was almost six feet with well-developed chest and arms. Eagle eyes looked to Magnas to give the signal.

The old chief raised his right arm and let it drop. The two opponents rushed for the knives. Colorado feinted as if to pick up his knife but instead hit Snake Eye with his shoulder, bowling him over. But, at the moment of impact, he too lost his footing and hit the dust. Desperately, both men scambled to their knees and in a crouching run dashed for the knives. Snake Eye grasped one fractionally ahead of Colorado and in a continuous movement tried to sweep it up into his adversary's gut. But Colorado, evading the stab, stepped in and picked up the other knife. Then he retreated nimbly to one side of the circle watching Snake Eye retrieve his full balance. The fight settled down after the first frenetic rush.

They circled each other in half-crouch positions looking for an opening, feinting blows to create one, waiting for a slip, a fatal lapse of concentration.

Snake Eye, eager to get at Colorado, made the first rush and, aiming for Colorado's body, tried a slashing movement. Colorado, however, stepped back, caught Snake Eye's knife arm and brought his own into action stabbing at Snake Eye's chest. But the latter was quick to react and grabbed the striking arm.

They stood there, each forcing his blade with all his strength at the other man. The crowd watched the deadly combat in silence, the taut straining muscles, the contorted faces of the fighters, fascinating them as they waited for one of them to give way and be despatched to the spirit world of his ancestors.

But it was stalemate. Each tried kicking at the other attempting to disturb his enemy's balance, but each was too quick or too strong. Colorado's mind raced for a solution, searching for an unorthodox move. Somewhere in the part of his mind that had detached itself from the grim threat which hovered over his chest, he remembered Brannigan's way of fighting. Using all his strength he forced Snake Eye's knife to one side and then releasing his grip on the knife arm hit out with a bunched fist. The blow landed on Snake Eye's nose, breaking it. Snake Eye's knife grazed Colorado's shoulder. Taking the initiative, Colorado pushed his opponent's legs from under him so that he hit the dust. Then Colorado was quickly on top of him, his big knees pinning both arms to the ground so that Snake Eye could not move them. His own knife was raised, ready to plunge downwards, to end the life of the Apache who had made him an outcast once again. But he held off and a low whisper rose amongst the onlookers who were pressing round the circle like buzzards waiting for the moment of death.

"Choose," he said to Snake Eye. "Life or death?"

"I choose to live." The voice was quieter but still hateful though humiliated. Colorado looked up at Magnas and waited.

"He chose life. Let him then live," the chief pronounced.

Colorado got to his feet slowly but Snake Eye leapt up.

"You made a mistake. You should have killed me as an Apache would have done. Your white blood shows again."

"I have proved myself your way," Colorado rejoined. "What could be more Apache than that? It is Snake Eye who cannot accept it." Murmurings in the crowd showed that some of the Apaches agreed and this angered Snake Eye further.

"From this day," he said, "I will live to kill you. There will be another time."

"Let your actions speak, not your words," Colorado replied. "That's what you would have of me."

Snake Eye looked at Magnas and then pushed his way through the crowd which began to disperse slowly now that the excitement was over.

When they had all gone Magnas and Colorado were left alone. The chief put a hand on his nephew's shoulder.

"You could stay now," he said. "You proved yourself and they respect you for it."

Colorado watched the remnants of the throng disappear. "But they will never forget that my mother was white. Snake Eye voiced the thoughts of many."

"You are your own man, Colorado, as are all Apaches. You must decide."

Colorado rubbed his jaw with his long fingers. "If I stay and the white eyes harass us, some Mimbreno will make much of my white blood. They will also remember that I am the nephew of Magnas. I wish to cause my uncle no embarrassment."

"I have lived with many troubles. One more will not cause me pain."

The old chief would have liked him to stay and Colorado knew it but he could see only trouble ahead if he did so. Snake Eye had been the first spark.

"I will go, uncle," he said. "For the reason I have given."

The chief's eyes dropped momentarily. He had lost all his sons and had been looking forward to having his nephew with him.

"You will always be welcome back. Remember that, Colorado, if trouble finds you again." He took the bear tooth necklace from his neck and Colorado bent forward as the chief slipped it over his head. "Always wear this," he said. "It makes you my son."

They walked back to Magnas's wickiup together and the chief sent for Colorado's horse. He mounted up, stretched down from the saddle and clasped the hand Magnas offered.

"Luck go with you," he said as they unclasped hands. He turned the horse, kicked it into action, and rode out.

Snake Eye, squatting amongst some rocks nursing his hatred and shame, watched him ride out. He was already wishing for the day they would meet again.

7

FORT BENSON was like many other forts in the southwest. Everywhere was heat and dust and glare of the pitiless sun. A rectangle of shabby adobes made up the tiny post. Officers' quarters, adjutant's office, sutler's store, the post bakery, commissary, quarter-master stores, blacksmith shop, corrals and stables were all of the stereotype.

Colorado rode in quietly. He had nowhere better to go. Since leaving the Mimbreno camp he had ridden the desert for three days, thinking, trying to decide his future. Eventually he had come to the conclusion that he could either hide all his days like an insect in the sand or be a man and go where he willed. He decided that a short life with his head held high would be better than a long life skulking in the corners of the desert lands.

Amongst the soldiers who peopled the fort, Colorado saw that there were some Apaches, dressed in various assortments of white men's apparel, many favouring the blue coat the soldiers wore. He figured that some were former reservation Indians, who, rather than face the dull life there, had chosen to scout for General Crook. Chincuahua, Tonto, Mescalero and even Mimbreno were represented. As he rode lazily through the fort their eyes watched him and he knew that some, undoubtedly, would recognise him.

Ahead he spotted the sutler's store with the sign hanging on a solitary pole. His thirst was powerful and by repute he knew this was the place it could be quenched. Dismounting, he tied his horse to the makeshift corral and entered.

He stood for seconds at the entrance surveying the scene before him. Someone at the piano in the corner was belting out a tuneless noise, whilst at the wooden bar civilians and soldiers were standing elbow to elbow. The laughter, which now and again would reach a raucous crescendo and then quieten again, was the laughter of the men who had drunk too much in a wild search for happiness, for an hour or two of relief from the monotony of fort life. Colorado heard it and knew it for what it was: superficial gaiety which could change its mood in seconds to cruel vindictiveness.

He unslung the Winchester from his shoulder and carried it low at his side as he moved quietly, catlike, to the bar. He stopped at one end, leant forward on one elbow and placed the rifle flat on the wooden surface. Nobody noticed him, being too engrossed in their own pleasures, until the barman looked along the line. Colorado saw the heavy frown line his forehead and simultaneously the piano stopped playing.

A big man, dressed in buckskin, who was standing a yard down the bar from

Colorado with his back to him, shouted, "Hey, Billy, watcha wanna stop fur?" The piano player stared back, looking over the big man's shoulder, causing him to turn.

The man's eyes met Colorado's, triggering the half-breed's memory. Many times he had seen the man scouting for the bluecoats. Once, unable to offer help, he had seen the man whip a sixteen-year-old Mimbreno to death and then take his scalp. The memory burned vividly like a firebrand and it was all Colorado could do to control himself.

The big man stretched to his full height and snarled into the silence which had gripped the place. "This place ain't for no injun."

Colorado, averting his eyes, fixed them ahead and made no movement. The only one who did move was the bartender who came along the bar towards the half-breed.

"One drink, injun, then you go," he said, pouring a whisky into a glass, hoping to avoid trouble.

"He don't get nothing, Joe," the big man emphasised the words, moving closer to Colorado and swiping the glass off the bar. The tinkle of the glass as it broke resounded unnaturally in the quietness.

Colorado turned his eyes lazily back to the man. Some of those present would have said he looked bored.

"I don't take orders from no man," he said, clipping his words. "Especially one who takes boys' scalps for fifty measly dollars."

Colorado's words spurred into the man, bringing red blood to his cheeks. When they were full up, his hands irresistibly went down to his holster. But before he reached it Colorado grabbed at the Winchester, took it in both hands and with a short clean stabbing motion, thrust its butt into the big man's face. He staggered back along the bar, into the men he had been drinking with, and then like a giant bull shot through the heart, collapsed on to the floor, holding his smashed face in both hands. The blood seeped through his fingers as he lay there but nobody moved to help him. Colorado reversed the Winchester so that he held it conventionally. His eyes roamed the room looking for movement but no one was stirring. Slowly he reached for the big man's whisky glass, picked it up and drained the contents. Then he began to back out of the room, watching the crowd. At the entrance he felt for the door but straightened when a cold barrel jabbed into his shoulder blade.

"Git 'em up," a voice demanded as hands came round and relieved him of his Winchester and Colt. Colorado responded, turning slowly to look into the faces of two soldiers who were covering him. The watchers remained silent.

"Jail's over there," the sergeant said, jerking a thumb over his shoulder and moving aside to allow Colorado's passage.

Colorado started walking while behind,

the noise in the room, revitalised by the incident, found its former momentum. But he felt nothing for the victim or the crowd. He'd stood up for himself as he'd vowed to do wherever trouble found him, regardless of the consequences. They could all go to hell.

Inside the low wooden building which served as a jail the corporal locked him in a cell which was bare except for a bunk bed, one blanket and a jug of water. When he was alone he lay down and relaxed. Whatever they decided it wouldn't bother him; life or death were equally acceptable to a man with no home, no place to go.

One hour later he heard the sergeant's heavy footsteps and opened his eyes.

"On your feet, injun," his jailer snapped. "General Crook wants to see you. Heaven knows why."

"He can go to hell and back," Colorado said matter of factly, rising languidly from the bed.

The sergeant made no reply as the

corporal joined them. Together they escorted the half-breed at gun point over the dusty parade ground to the Company Headquarters.

When they were inside, a captain rose from his desk, knocked on the general's door and announced that Sergeant O'Hara had arrived with the prisoner.

8

"SEND 'em in," a gravelly voice boomed and the sergeant pushed Colorado towards the door. His casual entrance contrasted with the snappy military coming to attention of the sergeant and corporal.

General Crook, who was writing at his desk, looked up and scratched the back of his head, assessing the Apache from a pair of lively young blue eyes which belied his grey hairs.

"You two can go," he said to the two soldiers who immediately exchanged rapid sidelong glances.

"Begging your pardon, sir," O'Hara spoke up. "This man's dangerous, sir."

The general drifted his eyes back to Colorado briefly and then lowered them back to his paperwork.

"He won't bother me, O'Hara," he stated. "You both can go."

The soldiers marched out leaving Colorado standing there untied and free to do as he liked. His eyes searched the room looking for a weapon, but, strangely, the general ignored him, continuing to write. The half-breed's curiosity grew, diverting him from thoughts of escape. He was certainly different, this soldier, to sit there so calmly.

Finally the general put aside his papers and eyed the half-breed.

"Smashed Bill Tidy's face with a rifle butt? That right?"

"He had it coming," Colorado assured him.

The general picked up his quill pen and stroked the feathers. "Which tribe are you from? Chiricuaha?"

"Mimbreno. My mother's white so I'm not Apache or white." He wondered why he'd added the last sentence.

"Tidy's had it coming a long time," the general said. "He needed taking down but by all accounts you took it a bit far."

Colorado inwardly registered surprise that this man was siding with him and wondered why.

"You lived with the Mimbreno?" the general asked and Colorado knew then he was leading somewhere.

"Once I did. Now I don't," he replied, not wasteful of words, and the general, taking the hint, came to the point.

"I need Apache scouts," he stated sitting back. "Got some. Need some more. You can work for me if you like. Pay's fifty dollars a month with two horses thrown in."

"So that's it," Colorado thought. "That's what he's been leading up to."

"No thanks, General," he was quick to reply. The general sat forward and stroked his chin.

"Can you tell me why not?"

"I'll never go back to the Mimbreno but I'll never betray them either," he stated simply.

"You won't have to," the general

explained. "You can avoid any mission against the Mimbreno, and I give you my word."

His answer made Colorado think hard. He felt that trailing other Apache hostiles wouldn't be so bad. There was no love lost between branches of the Apache nation; sometimes Apaches fought other Apaches. Apart from that he had to do something to avoid the boredom of wandering the desert alone. The pay sounded good too so he decided.

"I accept then."

"Good." The general rose from his seat and offered his hand. "What's your name?"

"Colorado."

"Well, Colorado, tomorrow you can join the five scouts who will ride with Lieutenant Masterson. They're going after Chief Chunte and his Tonto Apaches. Okay?"

The half-breed nodded his understanding and the general called in the sergeant.

"Show this man where the Apache scouts are quartered," he commanded. "He'll be joining us as from tomorrow."

"Yes, sir." The sergeant sprang to attention. Colorado followed O'Hara out of the building on to the parade ground. As they crossed it, the half-breed picked out a figure slumped against one of the adobe buildings, holding a bandage to his face and mopping it.

"I'll be looking for you, injun," Bill Tidy's voice roared. Colorado kept on walking.

"You've made an enemy there," O'Hara told him, his tone unsympathetic, almost gloating as they climbed the wooden steps to the long low building which housed the Apache scouts.

Inside it was clean with the beds arranged in neat rows. At the end, round the stove, some Apaches were sitting on chairs or lounging on beds.

The sergeant led him down the aisle and indicated one of the spare beds.

"That'll do you," he said bluntly. "You can get your weapons from the jail later."

He left Colorado alone with the Apaches who did not move to welcome him, so he lay down on the bed and shut his eyes until a shadow fell across him. He opened one eye, saw the Apache standing at the end of his bed, and opened the other eye. The Indian was of medium build, with long lank black hair riding free round his shoulders. A scar running down his left cheek met a slit of a mouth to give him a mean look.

"Why are you here, Colorado?" he grunted. "Many times I saw you with your uncle when he visited the Tontos."

"For the same reason as all are here. Tomorrow I will scout for the bluecoats."

The Tonto brave looked from Colorado to the others who were coming nearer now. "But your mother, she's white. You both left the Mimbreno.

Now the bluecoats have sent you to spy on us when we ride against Chunte."

The other Apaches murmured amongst themselves. Colorado knew that once again, as was becoming customary, he would find it difficult to fit in.

"I have come to scout against all tribes except the Mimbreno and not to spy," he stated plainly. "Is it not your loyalty which is questionable? You are Tonto yet tomorrow you will ride against your own people. Which Apache can do this?"

The other Apaches muttered. Colorado and the Tonto knew that the purport of the muttering was that the half-breed's words were true.

The Apache scowled down at Colorado's still reclining figure, turned angrily on his heels, and stormed off.

Colorado shut his eyes as the others dispersed. Yet again his caste had made him the man in the middle, the raw meat on which suspicion fed. Potentially, too, he had made another enemy in the Tonto Apache.

9

WHEN the sun rose next morning Colorado and five other Apache scouts stood on the parade ground watching 'C' troop form up for inspection.

Lieutenant Masterson, sitting arrogantly astride his white horse, rode up and down the lines. Colorado watched him carefully and saw in his manner a fussiness he did not consider manly. He knew the soldiers needed discipline, but this man's inspection was too fastidious, too concerned with irrelevant detail. A hard trail, not a Sunday Church parade, lay ahead.

"He is too young and foolish, that one," an Apache standing next to Colorado announced to the others. "He lacks the patience of the hunter. Look at his horse. It's too frisky, uh!"

"You can tell much about a man from the horse he rides, sure enough," Colorado rejoined. "The horse becomes like the man sometimes."

When he had finished his inspection, the Lieutenant galloped his white horse to where they were standing and pulled up in a cloud of dust. The horse reared up, whinnied, and then settled.

None of the Apache scouts moved or altered his expression as the Lieutenant studied them, his eyes moving rapidly from one to the other. Colorado figured those darting eyes reflected the man's character; too eager, too frenetic by half.

"You will leave us at the Daglish ranch," he told them imperiously, sweat already running down his young face. "The folks there reported seeing 'paches two days ago so you'll look for sign."

Nobody answered him. There had been an arrogance in his voice and manner though his words had been harmless enough. Each Apache had known by a long-developed, bitter sense of such things, that this man did not like him and considered Apaches as low a form of life as you could find. So when his words met sullen silence, he spun his horse and galloped back to the column.

They rode out then, the Apaches on foot running at a steady trot. The oppressive heat didn't worry them. Since boyhood they had been trained for such conditions and it was not unknown for an Apache to cover seventy miles per day on foot if necessary.

Colorado found himself alongside the Tonto who had baited him the previous night. Occasionally their eyes met and Colorado could see resentment still smouldering there. He knew the Tonto's name was Scar and he wondered who had scarred his soul, reflecting that perhaps the mark on his face told the tale.

When they were two miles out, one of the scouts pointed ahead to a wisp of smoke curling lazily on the horizon. Scar ran ahead to stop the column.

"What does it mean?" the Lieutenant snapped.

"I would say it meant the 'paches have visited the Daglish ranch, Lieutenant," Sergeant O'Hara answered and spat into the dust near Scar's feet.

Colorado heard the reply and studying the Lieutenant's face saw not sorrow or concern in his eyes but speculation and greed. He had seen his chance for glory rising with the smoke ahead and drew his sword.

"We'll go full gallop, men," he shouted aloud.

The old sweats in the company exchanged cynical, knowing glances. They knew from their experience of desert fighting that you had to be wary where Apaches were concerned. The smoke could mean a trap and, if it was, the shavetail Lieutenant would lead them right into it.

Nevertheless, when the officer's sword prescribed its fancy arc and pointed ahead, like good soldiers they responded. They went ahead recklessly, at the gallop, leaving the Apache scouts behind in their dust.

Half an hour later, when the scouts caught up, they found that luckily there had been no trap but that, in any case, the mad charge had been in vain. They had known that would be the way of it. The soldiers were standing around disconsolately, watching the last of the hungry tongues of flame devouring the innards of the ranch-house.

The Lieutenant and O'Hara had organised a burial detail and the digging was in process when Colorado and the Apaches reported to him. At first, oblivious to their presence, the officer was staring down at the mutilated bodies while his men dug the graves.

Colorado, following his gaze, studied the bodies and saw that none of the whites had died easily. The family, man, woman and boy, had been mutilated with knives until their faces were unrecognisable as those of human beings.

The sound of the Lieutenant being sick dragged his gaze from the carnage and back to the soldier. The officer was flapping with his gloves at the vile puke which covered the front of his tunic and his hands were shaking.

When he had cleaned himself his eyes came up and self-shame flickered in them for a second until he saw the Apaches. Then the look became hateful.

"Devils," he yelled, "Black coon devils."

One Apache, fearing the worst, began to raise his rifle but Colorado restrained him and stepped forward.

"I see Apache women with their limbs cut off and still living," he stated coolly. "White men did it too."

Masterson locked eyes with Colorado for seconds and then the hate which had been a mask for his own fear subsided to leave only his arrogant distaste of the scouts. Suddenly, looking away, he stubbed his toe violently into the sand and crunched a spider which was scuttling for cover.

"Look for tracks," he mumbled. "Find out which tribe of coons did this."

At that, they spread out and covered the area looking for sign. Colorado picked up an arrow, examined it and saw from the colour of twine round the shaft that it was one of the Tonto tribe's.

Then Scar called them to him and they gathered round.

"Tonto moccasins," he stated triumphantly, pointing to some prints he had found and they all mumbled their agreement, noticing too the arrow in Colorado's hand had confirmed it.

Scar told the Lieutenant and pointed across the desert westward towards the horizon and the Dragoon mountains. That was the way, according to the tracks, the Tontos had ridden.

The officer, itching to get going, away from the bloodshed he had witnessed in this place, ordered the men to mount. Soon they were heading out towards the Dragoons.

For ten miles the column moved in silence except for the creaking of saddle leather and the clink of bridles. The troopers, perspiring heavily as the sun beat down, rode doggedly on, always aware that ahead lay the Apaches and possible death. More than one wondered if it was all worth the impecunious wage the army paid him. Maybe abject poverty back east was better than having your hair hang from an Apache belt.

At last, tired and dust-covered, they reached the foothills. Masterson, because he was tired himself, ordered a rest.

They fed their horses then dug into some hardtack washed down with coffee. Scar approached the Lieutenant and stood in front of the soldier who was sitting with his back against a rock. His mind was still going over the horrific sight he had seen at the

Daglish ranch so when he stared up at Scar there was still scorn in his eyes. But Scar, intent on other things, did not see it.

"Let me scout ahead, Lieutenant," he asked. "And maybe I can find them."

"You think you know where they are?" There was more interest, less scorn, evident now in the Lieutenant's voice and demeanour.

Scar smiled. "An old cave they use sometimes. It is not far."

The Lieutenant rose to his feet. "Go ahead then and find them," he said.

Scar turned away but as he did so the soldier had a sudden thought, a sudden suspicion.

"Why would you turn on your own?"

Scar faced him again and pointed slowly to the scar on his cheek.

"The old chief did that," he said bitterly. "That is my reason."

He turned away again. The Lieutenant watched him break into a half-run and disappear into the rocks. He too knew what it was like to hate and he understood that, for certain, Scar would not betray them.

An hour later that certainty was confirmed when Scar trotted back into camp. With gloating pleasure he told the Lieutenant that he had found the cave and that the Tontos were indeed occupying it. The sentries on the approach route would have to be removed however. But the Apache scouts could take care of that, according to Scar, and Masterson agreed that they could go ahead and do it.

So Scar, taking charge, broke the scouts into two groups and indicated roughly where Chief Chunte always posted his sentries. When they moved off, leaving the troopers, Colorado went with one of the Mescaleros. The soldiers would follow later at a snail's pace.

The half-breed and the Mescalero progressed slowly, senses honed to a sharp point, moving with stooped carriages, studying the ground. They knew that ahead was a pair of sharp eyes.

Colorado saw the deer-track first and pointed it out. The Mescalero nodded his understanding, knowing why it made the half-breed suspicious. For some reason the animal had left its easy course and veered off left uphill. Maybe a cougar, somewhere ahead, had caused that sudden diversion, but yet again, the chances were that it could have sensed the presence of man.

"I'll work high up to the right. See if I can get above him if he's there," Colorado told Mescalero. "You give me time."

The Mescalero's low grunt indicated he understood.

With lithe animal grace Colorado worked his way forward and up, making use of any available cover. When he figured he was high enough, he flat-bellied and peered down into the lower valley.

It was easy from his high position to pick out the Tonto Apache sitting cross-legged on a table rock some hundred feet below. His head was drooping on his chest and his rifle lay a few yards away. The brave was being careless probably because in the past the cave had been so safe for his tribe.

Looking back, Colorado caught a brief glimpse of a brown body moving between rock cover. The Mescalero had begun to move forward and it was time for him to move too.

Noiselessly, he worked his way down, leaping from rock to rock with cat-like stealth until he reached the shadow of the big rock where he was completely hidden from view. His strong fingers found handholds and he hauled himself upwards towards the sentry.

At the top he took his knife from his boot and put it between his teeth. Then he peered over the edge and simultaneously the sentry rose from his sitting position and stared down the valley. The Mescalero had been spotted and Colorado took advantage to haul himself up on to the top of the rock.

Gathering himself, his eyes never wavering from the Apache's broad back, he took the knife from his teeth and edged forward on his toes. A foot away, the Tonto's sixth sense told him something wasn't right and he began his turn. But it was never completed. Colorado's free arm, like a striking snake, shot out and encircled the Apache's throat. The Tonto dropped his rifle and grabbed for the arm but there was no time for him now. Colorado's other hand plunged the knife between his ribs, going deep. The Apache struggled for a while and then, when the life went out of him, Colorado let him go. He slumped on to the hard rock face and lay still, bait for the buzzards.

Colorado bent over, wiped his knife on the buck's shirt and then stood erect again.

"You do not scalp, uh!" The voice from behind him biting the silence caused him to whirl, but it was only his hunting partner the Mescalero standing there. The man's eyes were fixed, not on Colorado, but on the dead Tonto.

The half-breed shook his head negatively and slipped his knife back into his boot.

"I will take his hair," the Mescalero announced and walked over to the body drawing his knife. He dropped onto one knee and began his work cutting the skin round the top of the Apache's head in a circular fashion. The intricate work finished, he opened the buck's mouth with his fingers and plunged his knife into that orifice and out through the back of the throat. That effectively pinned the head to the ground. Gripping the knife with one hand he took hold of the greasy hair and pulled. With a sound like sandpaper drawn over wood the scalp came off.

When he came up holding the scalp triumphantly, blood dripping everywhere, his eyes met Colorado's.

"Why this?" the half-breed asked. "You did not kill him. You cannot take his power."

The Mescalero's lower mouth hung open as he looked at Colorado. His looks showed he thought the question stupid.

"White men's dollars," he grunted, shaking the scalp to rid it of the blood.

There was no further conversation as the Apache attached the scalp to his belt. Colorado had seen white men scalp for money but never an Apache. Times were surely changing.

10

WHEN they got back they found that the other scouts had already reported. Colorado saw fresh scalps on their belts and no explanations were exchanged. The Tonto sentries had been despatched without doubt.

Scar went off ahead as the soldiers moved out again quietly. Now they were afoot, leading their horses, and nobody spoke. The occasional snorting of a horse or the laboured breathing of the men when the ground rose was the only sound as each man entered his private world and mentally prepared himself for what fortune might have for him up ahead.

A mile up a small canyon, Scar appeared out of some pinon trees and called a halt. His head went back, sniffing the air and soon all the party caught the smell of woodsmoke. It meant the cave and the Apaches were not far ahead. The taut faces of the soldiers told of the strain that knowledge brought.

Scar approached Masterson.

"Not far," he said, and pointed to a narrow trail which ran up the side of the canyon rising all the time until it disappeared behind a rocky outcrop. "Some men stay here," the renegade added, "and catch them if they run. It is the only way down."

Colorado saw the pleasure this knowledge gave Scar. A faint lascivious smile played across his mouth.

The smile on Masterson's face was almost a replica and Scar puffed out with pride, taking it to mean that the officer was pleased with him. It was his cue to continue.

"Send some up that way," he said, pointing to the other side of the canyon. "A trail will take them higher than the cave. They can shoot down from the other side."

"And drive them down here where I'll be waiting to finish the dirty scum," the Lieutenant gloated.

"Sounds a fair idea sir," O'Hara interjected. "I'll take some men up the far side if you approve, Lieutenant."

Masterson pondered for a moment, wanting to add a little to the plan, otherwise the credit for wiping out Chunte and the Tontos wouldn't sit so well on him afterwards.

"Sure, Sergeant," he added, "but Scar and some other men can go up this side to get above them. We'll have them three ways then."

"I'll organise it, sir," O'Hara said eagerly. "We'll pay back those devils for what they did at the Daglish ranch." His angry eyes focused on Colorado as he spoke.

It took no time at all for the sergeant to organise the groups. The men, sensing their advantage and figuring these Apaches might be easy pickings, responded quickly to his orders. Within minutes Colorado found himself following O'Hara up the far side of the canyon while Scar and others took the cave side. The Lieutenant below waited edgily like a scavenger waiting for the remains of the meat after the big kill.

When they reached the top of the high bluff O'Hara halted them and with his men following him, flat-bellied his way to the edge.

Colorado alongside them looked down and saw the cave about fifty feet below on the far side of the valley. Some women and children were cooking outside while a few of the men were sitting amongst the rocks. It was a picture of domestic contentment violated only by the presence of the hunters who watched them and thirsted for vengeance and blood.

"Perfect," O'Hara enthused. "They won't know what's hit 'em."

Colorado felt the irritation grow. Ambushing squaws and papooses had never been his style and his misgivings grew as he watched the soldiers check their rifles in preparation. When he'd signed as scout he'd expected to chase young bucks, not to slaughter innocents.

When O'Hara gave the command, the soldiers drew bead in unison and each held his breath waiting for the sergeant's order to pour death into the afternoon. When he gave it, eight rifles snapped at the still air, spitting their deadly venom into the canyon while O'Hara's voice resounded a hearty, "Give 'em hell, boys."

Each syllable grated on Colorado's nerves and he had to watch helplessly. One bullet took a woman in the chest and whisked her round like a top. Another Apache hit the ground and bounced convulsively as other bullets ripped into him. Meanwhile, the initial disbelief on the Tontos' faces gave way to horrific understanding and they made a mad dash for the cave.

One Apache stooped in his run to pick up a child who was tottering around bewildered. That action cost him his life. Eight bullets peppered his spine lifting him a foot in the air. Another bullet flattened the child.

Then, as if it had never been, the rifle fire stopped. The sun beat down and the smell of death hung in the air while the only sound was the elated cry of a sharp-eyed buzzard overhead. Colorado directed some of his disgust at the soldiers, some at the buzzard, but most of it against himself for being there and doing nothing.

"Shoot into the cave, boys," O'Hara shouted, his enjoyment of the easy pickings evident. "The bullets will ricochet at them varmints. Fire at will."

Reloading as keenly as O'Hara, the soldiers peppered the cave again, turning it into a wasps' nest of whining bullets.

If there was a lull it was short, and the whining was replaced by the crying and wailing of the Apaches whose limbs had been smashed by the bullets. Colorado couldn't stand that and he knew he had to act. He crawled backwards and rose to his feet, pointing the Winchester at O'Hara.

"Stop 'em now, Sarg," he commanded with slow emphasis.

O'Hara spun onto his back and seeing Colorado and the rifle levelled at his middle, he moved his rifle to one hand and held it wide of his body. His eyes widened in amazement.

"You crazy injun. What the hell . . . " But his protests trailed away when he saw hard ice frozen into the half-breed's eyes.

One by one the other soldiers turned on their backs, rifles held clear of their bodies. Like helpless, overturned crabs they stared at Colorado.

"Drop 'em," the half breed commanded, and the rifles clattered on to the hard rock as they responded. Viciously, taking his spite out, he kicked the guns over the ledge into the valley while O'Hara glowered at him.

"What the hell you playing at?" O'Hara barked, unable to contain himself.

Colorado made no reply but studied their faces hoping to find a glimmer of understanding in one of them, some concession to humanity. But he saw only thwarted sadism and fear of the rifle he held.

"There's women and children down there, you bastards," he screamed at them. "You're no better than scum-sucking pigs."

"They're gonna lock you up for a long time, breed," O'Hara rasped back at him, his voice trembling with suppressed anger.

"It'd still be worth it," Colorado stated, wondering what his next move should be and waiting for the anger in him to die so that he could think logically.

Then the high-pitched, ominous wailing rose out of the valley to add to his confusion, until he defined it as the Tontos' death-chant. Issuing from the very bowels of the earth it blocked out thought.

"When they finish their chant they'll charge right down the trail at the Lieutenant," O'Hara said accusingly.

Colorado moved to the edge of the bluff to get a better view but kept the soldiers covered.

"At least they'll have more chance that way," he answered. "And if they die it will be out in the open like men."

The death-chant was prolonged and ended in a crescendo of high-pitched screams. There was a moment of stillness and then, below, two dozen Tontos, half-nude and daubed in red war paint, erupted from the cave entrance, like demons from hell itself. Their curses echoed in the valley as they charged down the trail.

Scar and his companions chose that moment to show themselves on the cliff opposite and to shoot down into the melee below. The leading Tontos caught in the first volley went down and blocked the narrow trail for their companions.

Then Masterson, eager for action, led his men round the bend in the trail and blocked it. His leading men dropped to one knee and fired. The bullets coming from two directions were too much even for the charged-up Tontos and they broke up and headed back to the cave with the bullets hissing and spitting at their bare legs as they went. When the last Apache reached sanctuary a dozen of the tribes' best braves lays dead on the track.

"You bloody coon," O'Hara cursed when the firing stopped. He had no way of knowing what had happened and he was frustrated.

Colorado turned to him when a movement on the cliff opposite distracted him. He saw that the soldiers, under Scar's urging, had rolled a huge boulder to the edge where it was precariously balanced. When Scar dropped his arm the soldiers put their full weight against it. It tottered and then plunged.

Crashing onto the backward-sloping incline at the front of the cave, it bounced and then began to roll, gathering momentum, heading for the recesses of the cave and the remaining Tontos. Again the screams of the Apaches could be heard and a Tonto crawled out dragging an injured leg, one arm raised in an appeal for mercy. A bullet, however, ended his optimism. Colorado looked up, saw Scar, and imagined his satisfaction. Then another boulder rolled into view and Scar, arms gesticulating frenziedly, encouraged it. He would not be content, Colorado reflected, until the last Tonto lay dead. He wondered why none of the bluecoats was calling for surrender but realised how forlorn that hope was. They were almost as anxious as Scar to wipe out the tribe.

There was only one course of effective action left and Colorado took it. Putting the stock of the rifle against his shoulder he aimed at

Scar and pulled the trigger. The impact of a direct hit caused the Apache to stagger back a pace. He stood there on the bluff, one hand grasping the chest wound, the other stretched out in front of him groping like a blind man. Then he staggered forward and went over head-first. Transfixed, his companions watched him fall and then retreated for cover before they met the same fate.

Colorado knew that now was the time to give the Tontos the only chance they would ever get and called out in Apache. He told them there was no way they would escape and advised them to come out without their weapons, hands high. He figured the soldiers would hold off if they did that. Then he waited to see.

Minutes passed before the first Tontos stumbled unarmed into the light, shielding their eyes. When there was no immediate fire, others came out, warily, until there were seventeen in all, including women and children.

They took the trail towards Masterson, stepping over the dead bodies of their comrades. The Lieutenant let them come and Colorado started to feel better.

He thought he had succeeded in saving them but he had misconstrued the officer's intentions. When the unarmed Tontos were half-way down the trail and when there could be no turning back, Masterson gave the order to fire. The front rank of the Tontos dropped and the others, accepting their fate, fell to their knees like supplicants at an altar. In seconds, the soldiers' bullets had killed or wounded them all and Colorado turned away, regretting that he had persuaded them to leave the cave. A deep sadness hung over him then.

O'Hara, who had turned on his belly and sneaked a look, sneered at Colorado. "How you gonna get down now, injun?"

The words sliced into Colorado's

morbid thoughts bringing him back to his own immediate danger.

"You'll go down," he snarled. "I go the other way. I want to get as far away as I can from your stink."

He looked behind him and saw a trail which would lead him down into another canyon. It looked an easy descent and the canyon had several adjoining branches. He could disappear forever into any of them and lose the soldiers.

Bending over O'Hara, he grabbed his tunic and pressing the barrel of his Winchester in his gut, hauled him to his feet. Spinning him round he pushed him to the edge of the overhang.

"Lead your men the way we came but don't look back," he ordered. "I'll be waiting to see if you do."

He pushed O'Hara back amongst his men who were rising slowly to their feet. Grumbling and dusting himself down, the sergeant led them away to start the descent.

Resting his Winchester on his shoulder,

Colorado watched them go and when they were half-way down he began his own trail in the opposite direction.

He hoped he would never see the bluecoats again.

11

THAT night, Colorado set his camp in a thicket of mountain mahogany and prickly pears. That made it virtually impossible for any pursuer to creep up on him without some noise. He always slept lightly anyway.

His sleep was good and undisturbed. Next morning he rose with the sun and was on his way, determined to put as much distance as possible between himself and any Apache scout who might have been ordered to trail him. When he felt safe he would rest up, consider his future. Right now, as he loped along, he wondered if he had indeed any future. The world had become a smaller place for him again now that he had crossed the soldiers.

At noon he came to a ridge and topped it on hands and knees. What he saw below sent him scuttling backwards hoping that those he had seen hadn't spotted him. More cautiously, he crawled back and exposing only his upper head and eyes, surveyed the scene.

Three Apaches, bareback on their broncs, formed a triangle at the extremities of a basin-shaped hollow. A light wind occasionally stirred their long hair, otherwise they were motionless. In the middle of the basin was a wooden cabin and an adjacent corral.

Colorado's eyes, darting to and fro, caught a slight movement and zeroed in at the corral, to focus on a figure tied to the fenceposts. He saw that it was a man and that his body, strapped to the posts by leather thongs, was stretched as far as it would go, and bent into a bow-shaped arch. The belly, like a pregnant woman's, was thrust unnaturally forward. An Apache lance protruded from the ground, its point in the man's back.

Colorado knew that if the man

moved too much he would die. By now he would have lost much blood and the lance, so expertly twisted into his body, could not be removed without causing internal damage. It was a slow way to die, typical Apache torture. But why were those bucks spread out and waiting?

He moved his eyes around, straining to piece this thing together, until a flash of yellow amongst some rocks near the cabin caught his attention. He saw hiding there a yellow-haired woman, hanging on to a Winchester as if the very breeze could waft it away and leave her defenceless. Huddled against her, keeping low, was a small boy.

He knew now why the Apaches were waiting. They had chosen to come at her from three angles. She might get one of them but the other two would ride in on her. Colorado guessed that her husband had hidden her and she had broken her cover to defend him, possibly when he was being tortured.

If he was right, he figured she sure had guts.

Fleetingly it crossed his mind to ride on out of it. It wasn't his business. The woman was white but her attackers were classed as red men. He belonged to neither world as he was so often bitterly reminded. Recent events had gone against him and he had left enough trouble behind him. But his doubts passed quickly. There was a woman down there in bad trouble and his conscience told him what had to be done. That was all there was to it.

Obeying his conscience, he pulled his Colt from its holster and placed it on the ground beside him in readiness. Then he shouldered the Winchester and sighted it on one of the Apaches. It would be an easy shot for him. His target loomed large in his sights and he construed that he could probably squeeze off three shots before they could ride up the ridge to kill him.

He had begun to squeeze the trigger when he heard a familiar noise off to his left. Slowly he eased off the pressure and felt his heart beating faster as the rattle increased. He knew the sound well enough and it was near, so near that he hardly dared to confirm it as he swivelled his eyes in that direction. But the ugly head of the rattler, raising itself and flickering out its tongue defiantly, was unmistakably a couple of feet away from him, a horrible reality.

Fear generated fast thought. To reach for his knife would be fatal. The rattler would strike too quickly. He had no time, either, to bring his rifle round and aim it. The handgun was too far away to reach for.

He chose his last and only feasible option and in a sweeping motion of his arm thrust the end of the rifle barrel at the snake.

In a blur he saw the head snap forward and the tongue strike at the barrel. In the same instant he was diving at the handgun and rolling. As he came up out of it he aimed and fired. His awareness of the Apaches exaggerated the Colt's report a thousand times but he was relieved to see the shot blow the rattler's head apart.

There was no time now and he knew it. Those bucks had been warned. Dropping his Colt, he grabbed for the Winchester and scrambled to his feet. Below, he could hear the ominous beating of unshod hooves. When he reached the vantage point, they were halfway up the incline, digging their moccasined legs into their mustangs' flanks in their mad race for life. Up there on the ridge, a man had the advantage of them and they had to reduce the odds by getting to him quickly.

Colorado exposed himself to full view and brought the rifle up to his shoulder. He shot the nearest one at forty yards, putting the bullet right between his eyes. The Apache somersaulted backwards and hit the dust. His companions, driven to fury, kicked even harder but his next shot took his second target in the chest. He was close enough to see the crimson jet of blood spurting.

The third Apache, knowing he needed cover, reined in, leapt from his horse's back and dragged it round to cover him. He fired two shots under the animal's belly but missed while Colorado's quick retort brought the beast down. For a second the two men watched each other and each knew he was near to death as he would ever be. They drew bead simultaneously but Colorado squeezed first and his bullet hit his opponent in the shoulder knocking him over. The Apache's rifle was thrown clear and Colorado breathed easier knowing it was all over.

Slowly, the half-breed raised his Winchester to finish it. But something about the man's features registered at the back of his mind and he lowered the gun hesitantly.

Realisation dawned then and he cried out, "Natchez, is that you?"

The Indian rolled over and looked up the hill, holding the damaged shoulder with one hand.

"Do it, Colorado," the voice came back at him. "Prove yourself yet again an enemy of the people. Already you have killed Eagle and Chini."

Colorado glanced at the dead bodies of the other Apaches and made his voice dry when he spoke.

"You act for Magnas?"

Natchez looked at him slyly. "Magnas has grown old. We ride with Snake Eye now."

The answer did not surprise the half-breed. At White Springs he had sensed some dissension amongst the rank and file of the Mimbrenos. Snake Eye would have been behind that and now he had broken away.

"How many ride with Snake Eye?"

"Thirty. All young men," Natchez grunted.

Colorado went over to him, put an arm under his good shoulder and helped him to his feet. When he was steady the Mimbreno looked at him incredulously.

"You let me live, uh?"

Colorado didn't like the sarcasm in the voice.

"I only kill to protect myself and maybe women and papooses. This a Mimbreno would not understand."

Natchez did not understand and eyed the half-breed slyly knowing that today Colorado would not kill him. The moment had gone.

"You make another mistake," he said. "First with Snake Eye, now with me. You know I'll be back."

"We live by different codes. Go while I allow it."

Natchez didn't need further bidding. Colorado watched him stumbling away, relieved that at least he was on foot. That would gain valuable time. He stooped to pick up a bow and arrow.

Then he remembered and caught a movement below in the basin. He saw the woman making for the corral. He walked down to her, past the dead bodies, and halted a few yards behind her. She was staring helplessly at the tortured body on the lance while the boy's face was buried deep in her skirts, hiding from the horror. Already, to Colorado, they looked lonely, deprived, and the scene moved him deeply. He knew their desperation and wanted to end it for them.

"Only a bullet will do it, ma'am," he said quietly, knowing he was stating the obvious.

She turned to him then and clutched the boy tighter. When he saw the intermingling of fear and pain in her face he realised she wasn't sure of him. He figured his Apache looks wouldn't help.

"Those three are dead," he reassured her, gesturing over his shoulder with his rifle. "And I'm sorry, ma'am, but it would be better for him if he was too."

He pointed to the man on the lance whose head was hanging loosely on his chest. His whimpers low and soft were those of a child newly born, sad and forlorn coming from a man full-grown. The man's mind had gone beyond sanity into a realm where his terrible pain was just commensurate with life.

Colorado looked down at the boy who was studying the half-breed through tear-misted eyes. He saw that the youngster, who was around nine years old, was half Mexican and surmised that the man on the lance would be his Mexican father. Behind the tears, the big brown eyes pleaded with Colorado and the breed knew that, young as he was, he understood that there was only one way to end the suffering.

"Do it quick," the woman said, making the decision and pulling the boy closer to her. Without leaving time for more thought Colorado aimed the rifle and fired. The rifle's report was as sudden as the woman's decision and as it echoed the woman and boy clutched each other more tightly. The breed turned away from the scene, feeling helpless, and ushered his two charges back towards the cabin. Nobody turned back now.

He sat them on the wooden steps of the cabin wondering if they'd be all right. For the first time he noticed the woman was good-looking with pale skin, blue eyes and yellow hair but right now she was two shades paler than on her best day. He left them there and started towards the barn figuring they'd want to be alone for a while. But he hadn't gone ten yards when he heard footsteps and felt something grab his right leg and hold on tight.

Looking down he saw it was the boy who had come after him in a rush and in his face, as he stared concernedly up at Colorado, was an unspoken plea for protection. Maybe it was because they were breeds but in that moment both sensed, though they could not have analysed it, strong affinity. Colorado stroked the boy's hair reassuringly, and at the same time his eyes met the woman's.

"He's better off, kid," he said,

bending down and putting an arm round the boy's shoulder. "He'll never grow old like you and me. We only grieve for selfish reasons." He said it for both of them and wished he could have said more. But what could you say to a young kid about death?"

"He was my pa," the boy said in a whisper as Colorado picked him up in his huge arms. There wasn't much else he could do but hold him there. He'd said all the words he knew.

"You got horses, ma'am?" he asked, forcing his mind to think practically.

"In the barn," she said, lethargically, and he knew she was still in shock.

Carrying the boy he went into the building and found two horses. To take the youngster's mind off his pa, he got him to help him saddle them and they each led one horse out and over to the woman. He picked up the bow and arrows and tied them to the saddle.

"We ain't got long, ma'am," he said. "Got to get going now."

She stood up mechanically and climbed stiffly into the saddle while Colorado bent down, scooped the boy up and sat him on his horse. Then they rode out at a canter.

Colorado knew his plans would have to change. Alone, Snake Eye would have probably never found him. But now, when Natchez told his tale, his enemy would know he would head to the fort with the woman and boy.

But he figured they had a good chance. He'd filled three water bags before they'd set out and guessed it was two days' hard ride to the fort. Given luck they could make it.

He made up his mind he wouldn't push the horses yet. If Snake Eye did catch up they'd have to run for it. Since these horses could outdistance the plodding Apache broncs if it came to a sprint, he'd save them for that. With this in mind, periodically he ordered the woman and boy down and the three of them would walk.

On those occasions the boy held

Colorado's hand while he walked beside him. It gave the man a strange feeling. Nobody, except maybe his mother, had been dependent on him before. He decided he liked the feeling.

The woman had been silent for long periods but she eventually came out of herself and asked him if he was Apache born and bred.

"Half-breed ma'am," he replied. "Those dead fellers back there were Mimbrenos from my old clan."

He saw her eyes widen with surprise and noticed that she was scrutinizing him more carefully. In fact, she was understanding now the magnitude of what he had done for the boy and her and the consequences for him.

"My husband was a Mexican," she said, more composed though the slight tremor in her voice told Colorado the effort she was making. "We married young," she added wistfully. "I was just seventeen and he was the only man I knew who was half-decent."

"You got brother and sister, ma'am?

Someone to take you in?"

"My folks died way back. I was an only child."

"You'll be all right," he found himself saying. Her innocent look and lack of outward self-pity had got to him and he felt the need, however weakly, to comfort her.

She looked at him quizzically and he averted his eyes. He was a kind man she thought. Diego, her son, had a way of sensing such things and had taken to him. On his part, for a big man, he was gentle with the boy and she sensed the bond between them, the unspoken empathy. It pleased the mother in her.

Always she had protected her son. She had heard rough white men call her husband a greaser in front of the boy, provoking his manhood. She didn't want her husband humiliated nor the boy to lose respect for his father so they lived out here in these wild lands. It had been her idea. She'd never trusted strangers but she had faith in this half-breed who'd come out of nowhere when she'd needed help. If there was a God, He'd answered the prayers she'd offered when she was trapped in those rocks, waiting for the attack.

12

NOON found them walking up a high ridge. Colorado topped it and pulled the horses and his charges back quickly. He tethered the horses and the three of them crawled back up. Six hundred yards away there was an overturned stagecoach, the two dead horses still in their traces, and four Mimbreno Apaches poking amongst the baggage with their war lances. One of them scooped up a gaily-coloured woman's hat and rode round proudly showing it off to his companions. The sound of their laughter at his antics carried across the flatland but brought no mirth to the three watchers in the hills.

Far off in the distance, imperceptible except to the trained eye, Colorado saw the dust cloud. Watching it move, he knew it was formed by a small group of people who were walking.

"There are no bodies, no passengers?" The woman was questioning him, breaking his concentration.

"They've gone," Colorado replied, pointing in the direction of the dust cloud he'd seen. "That way."

"What happened here?" Her voice was unnaturally high-pitched because her fear was returning.

"Those 'paches surprised them, ma'am, killed the horses for food I reckon. The passengers got clear and started walking."

"Are they safe?" She wanted reassurance but he didn't give her any.

"They figure," he said, pointing at the four braves, "that they've all the time in the world. Those people are on foot now."

As he spoke his eye caught another movement of dust in a different direction. This time he knew it was one rider and as the figure neared and took form he postulated from the style of riding that it was another Apache.

Eventually the horseman reached the stagecoach and the Mimbrenos gathered round him in a tight cluster, gesticulating with their arms in response to whatever he was telling them. Then, suddenly, as one body, they rode off in the direction from which the newcomer had come. All below was still. The stagecoach, like a once-powerful, now fallen giant who has lost his attraction, lay as still as death itself.

When the Mimbrenos' dust was miniscule on the horizon, Colorado mounted up and rode down, the woman and boy following on behind. He rode up to the coach, dismounted and searched for signs.

It was easy to piece together. The Apaches had chased the coach until it overturned and the passengers had abandoned it to take shelter amongst some small boulder formations. Then they'd started walking. From their shoemarks he noted that two of the party were women and one of them was being helped along by a male. There were four other sets of bootmarks and two of those were made by the boots the military usually wore. Colorado didn't like that.

Finished with the signs, he wondered why the Apaches had departed so suddenly. More than likely Snake Eye had recalled them. One good reason for that suggested itself; Natchez had found his chief and he was preparing to ride out and find Colorado with his whole band.

The woman came over to him with Diego and he explained to her what had happened, occasionally referring to the tracks. When he'd finished she fixed him with her big blue eyes and he swam in their innocence until she asked the question he didn't want to hear.

"We're going after those folks, aren't we?" Only the colour of his skin hid the flush in his cheeks when he answered, "Didn't figure to, ma'am."

Then his eyes flitted from the mother's to the son's and read there that the youngster understood what the woman was asking, the implications too. Together their eyes pierced his hard shell like arrows going straight to the fleshy part of a cactus.

"Suppose we'll have to," he added, retrieving himself against his instinct. The military men in that party would only spell trouble for him. He cursed himself for the power that mother and boy had over him. They had challenged his manhood and he'd risen to it, wanting them to think well of him. He saw the relief on the woman's face.

As they rode out following the trail, each yard covered was in the wrong direction and reduced their chances. But the die was cast, or had been cast for him, and it was no good looking back.

13

"RIDERS coming, sir," Sergeant O'Hara croaked hoarsely to Lieutenant Masterson as he glanced over his shoulder at their backtrail.

Masterson halted, swung round, and wiping the sweat from his hands on his tunic, raised his field-glasses. The other members of the party with him, screwing up their eyes against the sun, staring anxiously at the approaching riders dreading that they might be Apaches.

"One of them's a woman," the Lieutenant informed them, passing the field-glasses to O'Hara. The tension amongst them visibly lifted then.

"It's that dam injun, sir," O'Hara said, lowering the glasses and instinctively drawing his Colt.

The Lieutenant's face contorted into

a mask of hate at O'Hara's words and he unbuttoned his holster.

"He's come back to me sooner than I thought," he rasped.

They waited for the riders and when they reined in the officer drew his gun and pointed it at Colorado. His anger made his hand waver but Colorado looked unflinchingly down into the muzzle and then beyond it into the Lieutenant's young face. The lack of fear in the half-breed unnerved Masterson. Never before had he come across such disdain at gunpoint and it surprised him.

"Well! Well!" he said, finding his voice. "You find all kinds of varmints in the desert I guess."

The woman, seeing their eyes locked in hate, was puzzled.

"He came to help you," she said. "All of you."

O'Hara laughed at her and stepped forward to take the bridle of Colorado's horse. "This feller killed an army scout," he stated so that they could all hear.

The woman looked to Colorado again, wanting him to deny the accusation but his gaze was no longer on the soldiers. He was busy now assessing the other four members of the parry who had been listening mutely to the conversation. The soldiers were just wasting words. Snake Eye was the real danger now and nothing in the past or present would count if he caught up with them. There would be only hell to pay.

He appraised the two women, noting the stark contrast in appearance. One was a delicate, skinny creature who wore the latest fashion in dress and shoes. The other, more rugged and buxom, wore a shirt and trousers with the legs tucked into boots. The skinny one was hanging on the arm of a curly-haired, fresh-faced young man. Both man and woman looked at Colorado and he saw in their faces disgust for him checked only by a natural fear.

His eyes shifted to the older man of the group whom he marked down as the driver. He looked the dependable type; too old to have a hot temper and to have lived that long.

He concentrated on the third civilian and it was he who bothered him most. His lean build and steady eyes made Colorado think of a black panther resting but all the time aware of everything going on. There was a self-possession about him and the half-breed decided that nothing would be half-way with the man. There would be no nuances; he would be either big help or big trouble in any situation.

"He helped me, Lieutenant," the woman was complaining again. "And he killed three Apaches."

"You never know with his kind, ma'am," the Lieutenant explained. "They're as whimsical as mad dogs. It's the mongrel breed I guess."

"Where are your men, Lieutenant?" Colorado cut in, ignoring the insult because there were more important matters. His voice was demanding in spite of the gun pointing at him.

"Ambushed," O'Hara snapped. "Only me and the Lieutenant got away and we was lucky that the coach picked us up." He paused, "But then maybe you'd know all about that ambush, injun."

Colorado looked at him hard, aware of the stupidity of wasting time. Every minute could count.

"There'll be another nine dead pretty soon," he said, talking loudly enough so that the whole group could hear, "Unless you've got a plan those Mimbrenos will catch you easy."

"Feller's right," the grizzled stagecoach driver chipped in. "You have got a plan, Lieutenant?"

All eyes turned to the officer but his face was wooden and gave them little confidence in him. It was clear he had no plan beyond putting as much distance as possible between them and the Apaches.

"I can maybe help you all live a little longer," Colorado ventured casually, "if you do as I say." He was thinking about the women and boy more than the men's lives when he said it. The men could go to hell for all he cared.

"You've done your damage, breed," Masterson snapped back.

"I don't give a damn about you," Colorado came back at him. "Snake Eye can slit your gizzard for all I care."

The Lieutenant's lip began to quiver with frustration. His uniform usually meant instant obedience. He wasn't used to this kind of insolence and it galled him.

It was the buxom woman in the man's clothes who stepped in between them, hands on hips and looking from one to the other.

"I'm for following the injun," she said bluntly. "Any fool can see that the woman and child aren't with him for nothing." Her voice rose a pitch. "Besides, injuns know injuns."

"He's a traitor," O'Hara said obstinately.

The woman swung on him. "You're

military and the rest of us are civilians. I reckon right now we ain't prejudiced the way you are. Our lives are too important to us."

"You tell him, missus," the driver added. "What about that, Lieutenant?"

Masterson sensed the tide of opinion was going against him. Besides that, a cooler appreciation of the situation made him realise the woman was talking sense. Then there was his own skin to consider. The half-breed probably gave them their best chance much as he hated to admit it. Off the main stage tracks they could wander for days without knowing where they were heading. Then behind them somewhere were those Apaches. He shuddered at the thought of what they might do to his body. He still had not forgotten the Daglish family.

"Unfortunately I must consider the safety of the civilians," he said ponderously, the words leaving a bitter taste in his mouth. "We might as well be sightless as be out here with no scout."

He avoided O'Hara's eyes.

"But, sir, you know . . ."

"He'll be punished, O'Hara." The words were snappy, indicating he would brook no further argument about the matter.

It was good enough for Colorado, who began organising.

"Women and the kid ride the horses by turns," he promulgated. "The men can walk."

"Where we headed?" the old-timer asked, wiping his brow with a grubby sleeve. "I'm tuckered out now.

Colorado pointed ahead. "The mountains," he said sombrely. "Plenty of water there. I know a place."

"In which direction does the fort lie?" Masterson asked.

Colorado studied him, reading behind the question, and pointed in a different direction to the course he had suggested to them. The young curly-haired gent spoke up in a southern drawl.

"Then why don't we head that way, head for home?"

"Because they'd catch us for sure. If we make high ground, we can hold 'em a while, live longer."

"There were only four of them," the young man said sulkily. "We outnumber them."

Colorado felt his patience going. "There's more on the way," he said cursorily.

But the lilting southern voice droned on. "How do we know you won't deliver us into their hands? After all you're a coon yourself."

He said it as if it was the most natural thing in the world to say. He didn't consider it an insult, just a factual statement. Back home, he was used to ruling roost over the niggers, and Apaches he classified the same. The others knew this and watched the half-breed's reaction.

Colorado felt the heat inside him stoked by the arrogance on the youth's face but he turned away. The man was a fool and what lay ahead would sort him out; life would teach him a hard lesson. So he started to stride out. The southerner could do what he liked.

They all followed, including the southerner, and for an hour they plodded through the sand, stopping only occasionally to change the riders. When they reached the start of the foothills they were a bedraggled bunch, ghost-like, with their alkali-stained faces and dusty clothes.

Colorado had been watching their backtrail and knew Snake Eye was on his way. Intermittently he had seen the distant dust cloud. But he knew it was still an hour's walk to water and a place they could defend. The timing would be a close thing judging by the distance but he thought it just favoured the Mimbrenos.

He swiftly inspected the group and nagged them to get them going again. Instinctively he offered the young woman with the southerner his hand as she started to mount the horse.

Disdainfully, as if it was a dirty corrupt thing with no place in her life, she ignored it and climbed up herself. When she was seated she stared ahead, her eyes narrow and cold.

Colorado turned away shrugging indifferently. The woman and her son saw it happen and came to his side.

"Colorado!"

He looked down at her. It was good to hear her use his name softly like that. But he hoped she wasn't bringing him a problem, not now when it was vital to keep going.

"Ma'am?"

"I just want you to know me and the boy are grateful. I know twice today you could have ridden on. That woman, well she didn't know a gentleman when she saw one." She lowered her eyes as she paid him the compliment then went on. "My name's Liz. Maybe we'll be good friends."

He liked the shy way she said the words and he knew they were meant.

Something inside him reached out to her and the boy, some natural instinct to protect, to be responsible for them. Maybe afterwards . . . . But there was no time now. He smiled his thanks.

Colorado set a fast pace then and the others struggled to keep up. He hadn't mentioned the danger behind them. Panicking them he didn't think would do any good and in any case one of them would look back and notice soon enough.

O'Hara it was who saw the dust cloud first.

"They're coming," he yelled and the party stopped to look.

Colorado shielded his eyes, assessed their progress and cursed in Apache. Their destination, two seeps of water and the defensive cover around them, were at the head of the broad canyon they had entered. But, roughly measuring what lay ahead against the estimation of the pace of the war party, he figured they wouldn't make it. There would be about half a mile in it but that would be as good as eternity if the Mimbrenos caught them.

Apart from the southern woman who had begun to weep on her gentleman's shoulder, they had taken it well. So he set off again, forcing the pace and they followed much faster now, driven on by a more immediate fear.

He stopped them when they reached the point where the valley narrowed. It was the best spot for his plan. Though a mile from the seeps, nowhere else would be as good.

"We'll have to hold 'em up, buy time," he told them when they'd gathered round him, a new intensity about them now, realising they would have to depend on him.

"Some chance of that," O'Hara said to no one in particular. "There must be twenty or more of 'em from the dust they're kicking up."

Colorado ignored him. "I need someone, a good shot, to stay here with me while the rest of you go ahead."

His eyes roamed over them and fell naturally to rest on the silent man with whom, as yet, he had exchanged no word. He saw him consider before he stepped forward away from his companions.

"I'm your man," he said blandly and was offered no opposition. The aura of self-possession about him suggested nobody would argue with him about it. "The name's Gant."

Colorado nodded his acceptance of the offer and addressed the others.

"Keep going no matter what," he stressed. "The seeps and good cover are at the end of the canyon. There'll be a steep bluff at the back of you."

They were too tired to dispute anything and, led by the Lieutenant, dragged their weary limbs into action. Colorado felt something tug at his breeches and looked down at Diego.

"What is it, little one? Your mother waits."

Diego's eyes filled with tears. "You're going to die like my pa, aren't you?"

Colorado bent down and put an arm round the boy's shoulder, but was momentarily lost for words.

"You gonna waste time like that," Gant's words distracted him.

"That feller will take care of me, Diego," he said, making the sarcasm evident. "He knows how to use that gun of his."

"Diego!" The boy's mother was calling him and he reluctantly moved away from the half-breed. Colorado watched them go before turning to Gant.

"How do you figure this?" the white man asked, scratching his nose. The manner and the tone of voice suggested he considered this was just one more tight spot for him; no better and no worse than other times he had known. The half-breed was glad of that anyway.

Surveying the area around them, Colorado was pleased there was enough vegetation to serve his purpose.

"Collect galleto grass, brush, parts

of trees, anything that will burn," he said, gesturing expansively. "Pile it high in the canyon where the sides come close."

Gant looked at him quizzically.

"It'll burn good and scare their broncos," Colorado explained. "They'll have to go round it on foot."

"Then we run for it, uh!"

"That's the size of it," Colorado affirmed.

So without more talk they got down to it, working frantically against time. Twenty minutes later when they had scavenged all they thought would burn, they stood back.

"That'll hold 'em," Gant said, taking out a cigar and lighting it. He tossed the matches to Colorado and turned to watch the dust cloud. "How long we got?"

"Ten, maybe fifteen minutes."

Gant inspected the other side of the canyon. "Good cover there," he mused. "I'll take it."

"Mister," Colorado called after him.

"Find your own way back, uh? There'll be no stopping."

The white man waved his rifle in the air, consenting. "You too," he said, watching Colorado light the brush. But under his breath he muttered, "Make sure you get back real safe."

Colorado waited beside the fire, watching the flames growing and the Apaches coming. Their formless figures sharpened into detail as they neared and his sharp eyes could identify individuals. Snake Eye stood out clearly at the head of the band, urging them on.

With a last glance at the fire which was raging by now, the flames forming an impenetrable wall, Colorado took off into the rocks. Once he'd found a good sniping position he settled, pumped cartridges into his Winchester and waited.

Soon the Mimbrenos came charging up and reined in below, thwarted by the sheet of flame. Colorado could see them clearly in the whirling dust their horses had kicked up, and could hear them whooping their anger and frustration. Those who were really worked up kicked their mustangs towards the fire hoping a gap would magically appear. But the horses had sense and stubbornly fought away from the heat and deadly flames. Realising the folly of fighting it, Snake Eye dismounted and the others followed his example and gathered round him.

When he had given his orders, they broke up, scattering for the slopes intending to work their way round on foot. Intermittently they were hidden by the spurs but Gant and Colorado knew that, in minutes, the best guerilla fighters in the world would be coming at them.

As the first Mimbreno popped up Colorado squeezed off a shot. The bullet drilled into the victim's shoulder and spun him. But in a half-crouch he managed to scramble for cover yelling out a warning to his companions.

Others showed their brown skins then

but warily and not for long. Colorado's bullets ricocheted off the rocks pinning them down, buying precious time but doing little damage. Looking across the canyon at Gant he saw that he too was holding them. But for how long? The spasmodic appearances and short sprints were for one purpose; to fix exactly the position of their ambushers.

Eventually they began the decoy tactics so familiar to Colorado. One man would show himself and as Colorado fired at him three more would sprint towards him and then dive for cover before he could fire again. It was a fine art with them and he knew their numbers meant that inevitably they would get around him. The moment of retreat would have to be well-timed if Gant and he were to win the race to the head of the canyon and comparative safety.

He had killed two and wounded another when he decided the time had come. It was time for them to take their own chance for life. The others had had theirs.

"Now, mister," he yelled across and a wave of Gant's rifle told him the message had been understood.

They bolted simultaneously, gripping their rifles and pumping their feet against the hard rock. Leaping spaces, abandoning control and balance, they thrust their bodies towards the canyon floor.

Sliding and slipping they eventually converged in a cloud of dust and shale, recovered balance and drove against the softer earth. Their race for life was on.

Beside him, Colorado could hear the white man's heavy, laboured breathing and his curses whenever he stumbled. Neither man thought of what lay behind but concentrated on his destination ahead where hope lay. Gant felt a burning between his shoulder blades where he anticipated the bullet or the arrow which would bring him down. The sensation of the adrenalin pumping through his body, lent him speed.

Behind there was no gunfire. The only sound was their heavy panting, eerie and unnatural in the silence of the canyon. Colorado figured the Apaches wanted them alive.

As he reached a familiar bend, he calculated there were three hundred lung-bursting yards still to go and risked a look over his shoulder. The lead Apache was around forty yards back and when he saw the half-breed turn a big smile lit up his ugly face; the hunter could smell his prey.

Their chances, however, remained good until a hundred yards from safety Gant suddenly halted, gasping for breath. When he tried again he began to stagger and weave in all directions, his brain losing the battle against his body's demand for rest and succour.

Colorado had eased off and was looking back, facing a decision as the big Mimbreno closed on Gant, the smile disappearing and giving way to a grim blood-lust. Closing up, he launched himself at Gant's legs and brought him down while further back a second Apache yelled in triumph.

Colorado made his choice in that instant; throwing aside his rifle and drawing his knife he sprinted at the sprawling Apache. The big Apache's body went limp and sprawled across the white man's as the half-breed drove his knife between his shoulder blades. He hauled the dead man off, watching the second Apache closing in quickly. Keeping as cool as he could, he groped for Gant's hand-gun, felt the butt, and with a surge of relief pulled it clear of the holster. There was just time to cock the hammer and pull the trigger. The gun exploded into life and the bullet ripped upwards into the encroaching Apache's stomach. For what seemed an eternity he cradled his stomach and then he fell to one side.

Grunting with fresh effort, Colorado did not pause but hauled Gant upright, threw him across his shoulders and resumed his sprint. But the delay had allowed the other Mimbrenos to come within twenty yards and it crossed the half-breed's mind that if he was to die he would rather it wasn't rescuing a white man, especially this one.

Then the whine of a bullet and pained yelp somewhere behind gave him hope. More covering fire erupted from somewhere ahead and mercifully he realised that he was nearing the canyon head. Driving hard he covered the last twenty yards while the Apaches behind dropped off, thwarted by the gunfire.

When he burst through the rocks, strong hands gripped him and relieved him of his load. He squatted down catching his breath.

"You did well, son," the grizzled stagecoach driver told him and patted him on the back.

When he'd recovered, he stood up and, assessing the way the Lieutenant had deployed his men, found it satisfactory enough. He reflected that they had good cover and plenty of water and ammunition. All they lacked was food but he might be able to do something about that later.

"Big feller," Gant called out from the shade of a rock where he was resting. Colorado walked over to him, thinking how well he had done in the race until he'd collapsed. Not many white men he knew could have got that far against hardened Apaches.

"I'm grateful to you," Gant said when Colorado stood over him. "Maybe one day I'll repay you."

"Don't need repaying, mister. Don't want nothing from no white man," Colorado told him ungraciously. But Gant was unabashed.

"You never know, feller," he called after him as he walked away. "You'll never know when you might need me."

14

COLORADO was satisfied with the Lieutenant's placing of the men but was disturbed by the horses. They had simply been tethered to some thick brush. The Mimbrenos, he figured, would try to spook the animals. Not only would that deprive the whites of their possible means of escape, it would also provide the Apaches with a good meal of horsemeat.

So he spent some time collecting ocotilla branches and brush. When he had enough, he tied it all together, strung it between two rocks and led the horses into the natural corral that had been formed. Then he collected some galleto grass and mesquite and threw it into the corral for them to eat.

As he finished Liz came over to talk to him. The strange way she looked at him was embarrassing.

"Where's the boy?" he asked.

"Sleeping back in the rocks."

"Then maybe you should try to rest too."

"Will they come again tonight?" She ignored his suggestion and looked at the sky.

"Unlikely. They believe the souls of those killed in the darkness wander forever between the living and the dead."

"Tomorrow then?" She shuddered involuntarily.

"Perhaps. You can never tell with them."

The conversation was strained because all the time she was looking at him in that strange way which so discomfited him. At last she spoke what was in her mind.

"If we ever get out of this," she said, looking at her feet, "and if you're so inclined, me and the boy would ride with you. We'd like that."

Again, as before when the boy

had clung to his leg back there in the canyon, he was dumbfounded. Disappointed and shamed, she began to turn away. Finding his tongue, knowing his hesitation had been hurtful, he called out.

"I'm mighty flattered, ma'am. You and the boy would make any man proud and I don't reckon a feller could do better."

The glum expression she had assumed left her and a trace of a smile appeared. She looked at Colorado like a shy girl on her first date and momentarily he was tempted. But something deeper than his feelings for her bit hard into him.

"It could never be, ma'am, no matter how I'd like it."

"Why?" she retracted the incipient smile.

"'Cos I'm a half breed. Wherever I go trouble follows."

"We could go somewhere quiet," she said hopefully.

"I ain't hiding no more, nor backing

down. In any case there ain't nowhere. People are the same everywhere." He said it bluntly and with bitterness.

"My boy's a half-breed too. You could help him a lot."

"Best to find a white man, then folks will accept him better. By the time he's full-grown things could have changed."

"You're stubborn," she replied. "But the offer stands."

"I'll remember. It was the best thing anybody ever said to me."

He watched her walking away. Part of him wanted her badly, always had since the first time he'd laid eyes on her. But he knew his life would be a violent one; the turbulence flowed in his blood. A peaceable man would be better for her and the boy.

"Never took you for a fool." A voice from behind interrupted his thoughts and he looked round to find that the buxom woman had come up.

"You won't get many better offers. Couldn't help overhearing, being naturally nosy."

"No, ma'am, guess I won't."

She looked him up and down, measuring him with a well practised eye. "Worked in a saloon all my days," she stated. "Seen some men in my time and I can read 'em like a book. You're one of the best but you're as bitter as hell."

"I've got cause."

"Well I'm just being nosy, I guess," she sighed. "The name's Star and I've come to offer my services, non-professional of course. I'm as good a shot as any man."

Colorado took his gun out and threw it to her. He was surprised how easily she caught it.

"Over there, ma'am." He pointed out a position in the rocks for her. "And keep your head down."

He watched Star walk off, quite impressed, thinking she was a gutsy lady who'd lived a bit. He wished there were more like Liz and her in the world.

Then he took up his own position

from which he would be able to see right down the canyon when it was light. It felt good to take the weight off his feet and he had begun to relax when something disturbed a loose rock behind him. In one fluent movement he sprang to his feet, whirled and pointed his Winchester.

The curly-haired southerner froze in his tracks. Colorado relaxed and lowered the rifle when he saw him.

"Look here," Curly Hair said patronizingly when he'd regained some composure. "Why doesn't somebody ride out of here? They could get help and come back."

"'Cos there's a mess of Mimbreno peopling that canyon and they're just waiting for a fool move like that." His voice was strained because he disliked the man so intensely it was an effort to speak to him. "You maybe can't see 'em but they're there. Sure as hell they're there."

"Henry is an excellent rider, a champion in Alabama." The woman's softer voice came from behind her beau. But the tone was haughty; it was obviously an effort to speak to him. Back home she would never have held a conversation with one of the black men slaves on her daddy's plantation.

"That's true," Curly Hair went on. "I was rather good. Those savages would never catch me. Barbara here is a fine horsewoman too."

Colorado saw where he was leading but pre-empted him.

"Mister, I lived with those people and they're just dying for you to try it. You ever seen what they can do to a woman?"

Colorado saw the southerner clench his fists and draw his lips back over his teeth. They were the actions of a child about to throw a tantrum.

"So we're just going to sit here and wait for them, are we?" The words were accusatory and almost shouted.

"You'll live longer that way," Colorado said, turning his back and walking away to find another spot where he could have some peace. Behind him he heard the southerner muttering.

When he was alone again he turned their situation over in his mind and decided on balance that their chances weren't so good. They had plenty of water and ammunition. The men were all able to fight and their cover was pretty good. Some time he could sneak out and maybe get some food.

What bothered him most, on the negative side, was that they were boxed in by the Apaches and the sheer cliffs behind. Those cliffs would be almost impossible to climb especially with the women. As for Snake Eye, he could wait forever and never give up. So he consoled himself with the thought that at least they were all alive with some hope. If they had continued their previous wandering the Apaches would have caught and slaughtered them by now.

His analysis was interrupted by the whinny of a horse somewhere to his right and a wave of blackest pessimism engulfed him when he heard more noises. Running in the direction of his remuda and peering through the bad light, his fears were confirmed. His makeshift fence had been pulled down and the two southerners were astride horses. He drove his legs harder hoping he'd be in time to prevent their flight.

But it was too late. They were already spurring the animals forward when he reached the corral. In desperation he held up his arms, splaying them wide, hoping to scare the horses and force them back, but they drove out of the corral at him. He made a half-hearted lunge for one of the reins, missed and stumbled. A flashing hoof just missed his head as he rolled and when he looked up he saw them ride clear down through the rocks into the darkness.

"We'll be back folks," Curly Hair yelled out of the blackness.

Colorado picked himself up and rubbed his head. "Sure you'll be back fella," he mumbled, "but not the way you think."

The Lieutenant was the first to reach him.

"What the hell happened here?" he asked.

"We lost two," Colorado told him. "Southerners retreated."

The stagecoach driver came up and heard. "Bastards," he said and spat. "No wonder they lost the war."

Masterson looked downcast. "Maybe they'll get to the fort," he speculated. "Bring help."

Colorado didn't answer as he replaced the fence. He knew that neither man nor woman was worth a thought now. When he finished he left the others and was still angry because they had two less guns and two less horses.

Masterson approached the place where he was squatting and held out something.

"This here's a heliograph," he said, still not particularly wishing to talk to the breed except out of the necessity to save his own life.

Colorado took the object from him and examined it.

"It's just a mirror," he stated, unimpressed.

"The army use it for making signals. It reflects the sun. Maybe we can attract a patrol."

Colorado inspected it more closely, a flicker of interest coming into his face.

"Supposin' I could get somewhere to use it. How'd I know where the patrols would be?"

"I know the times when they ride and rough directions," Masterson answered. "You draw a map of the territory and show me where we are maybe that'll help us work something out."

Colorado picked up a stick and began scratching a rough map in the sand. He figured there was a chance that the mirror might come in useful and he couldn't ignore any idea that might bring help. When he'd finished, they pored over it, eyes straining in the moonlight while Masterson told what he knew.

15

WHEN the sun announced the dawn, the whites looked wearily down the canyon. At first sight, everything looked peaceful and still with no indication that, out there, somewhere, their enemies were hidden and waiting. Yet when their eyes adjusted and absorbed detail, they were given a grim reminder. A hundred and fifty yards down the canyon two naked white bodies stood out against the green of the giant cacti to which they were strapped. The way their heads hung low and jerked occasionally told the whites that the southerners had already been tortured to the point of delirium.

"Why don't they just kill them and have done," Liz said, sickened by the sight.

"Too easy, missie," the old-timer spoke up.

Colorado looked at them both. "It'll get worse," he said grimly. Liz looked at him appealingly. "Can't you help them?"

"With a bullet maybe."

The old-timer inspected him with screwed-up, knowing eyes. "It'll come to that," he muttered, shaking his head. "It'll come to that."

Then all they could do was wait, wondering if and when the attack would come. Colorado thought not for a while. They would wait to see if the sight of the southerners would crack anybody up, maybe lead to a foolhardy rescue attempt. If that didn't happen, the screams, which would eventually issue from them, would be a psychological weapon, a weakener. Apaches knew how weak whites could sometimes be under that kind of pressure whereas they were hardened to it.

The woman revived in the late morning and her low whimpering carried to them. The gent came round a half-hour later; his moans were deep and guttural.

As the sun crept up the sky the day got hotter until the canyon was like a furnace. At noon the sun reached its zenith and the whites dripped with perspiration.

With the coming of noon, the screams too reached a high-pitched crescendo. If they didn't look, it sounded like coyotes baying to the moon in unison except there was the knowledge that excruciating pain and not celebration was the cause.

As the rawhide dried and tightened, their already-wearied bodies were pulled against the sharp incisors at their backs. Then the screams merged into one long protest which varied only in pitch and tone as other pin-points of pain were discovered and brought fresh torment.

The watchers were helpless.

"Is there nothing we can do?" Liz asked, but nobody answered her.

Two seconds later two shots chased each other and the screaming ended.

They looked round and saw Colorado ejecting his Winchester. Nobody said anything.

The rest of the day was long and drawn-out and their nerves were stretched taut. Nobody saw an Apache but always there was the uncomfortable feeling of watching eyes. A hidden, antagonistic presence pervaded the valley and their thoughts as they awaited an attack.

But the hours dragged and no attack came. They sat in their own enclaves amongst the rocks and there was no conversation. They were thinking back, remembering the best and worst of life and savouring the happier parts, as if that would somehow enable them to hold on to life longer. The two dead bodies out there putrefying in the heat, limp spectres now, served as a constant reminder of the transience of their own lives. That was why the bodies were there; to horrify and eat away at their confidence.

Late that afternoon O'Hara left

his position and found his way to Colorado.

"What the hell are they waiting for?" he asked. His tone was that of a man completely bemused and his ill-feeling towards Colorado was forgotten.

Colorado's mouth traced a smile. "They want you to sweat, to worry. Then they'll strike." He looked up at the sky. "It'll probably be tomorrow. They know we'll be tired."

O'Hara looked at him dumbly, tried to think of something to say and then, frustrated, spun on his heel and walked away cursing.

When darkness began to fall Colorado made his way to the remuda and found his saddle. Luckily the southerners hadn't taken it. The bow and arrows which he had picked up at the woman's ranch were still tied to it so he loosened them. He'd need them now if he was going to catch them some food.

He found Masterson and squatted down beside him. The Lieutenant's face had lost its youthful appearance and he seemed to have aged ten years. The air of defeat about him didn't help.

"I'm going for food," Colorado informed him, "Sheep or something."

He had expected an argument from the soldier but there was only a nod of weary compliance. The pomposity had gone out of Masterson. Those were real thoroughbred Apaches out there this time, not cardboard cut-outs from the classrooms of West Point.

Colorado worked his way upwards, taking it slowly. They'd have men posted on the bluffs above but he didn't want to go that high. If he moved quietly lower down, he might be lucky enough to find a bighorn.

For an hour he searched, senses awakened to every sound that might announce one of his human enemies or the bighorn he required. Then ahead of him, prominent on a rocky outcrop, he saw the outline of a large ram and permitted himself a smile of satisfaction. He fitted an arrow and drew back the twine, hoping that when the ram fell its horns wouldn't catch the rocks and echo.

His aim was true and found the ram's heart but he winced as it toppled and scraped its horns against the rocks. Irritated, he sat down crosslegged peering out into the darkness, knowing he'd have to wait now to see if any Apache who had heard the noise would investigate. After ten minutes and no sign of any enemy, he toed it towards the animal.

When he reached it, he paused to look again and then bent over. Gripping the animal's fore and hind legs he hauled it upwards and draped it round his shoulders. But as he was straightening and adjusting to the weight, something cold pressed against his neck and he knew it could only be the barrel of a rifle. The shock caused him to take his breath in and he prepared for the worst.

"You are lucky it is I who finds you, Colorado," a soft voice, which he vaguely recognised, announced as the barrel was withdrawn.

Colorado turned his head towards the voice, simultaneously slipping the ram from his shoulders. His eyes, when they focused in the darkness, recognised Raven Wing, Snake Eye's squaw.

"You have forgotten me," the girl said coyly when he had not immediately spoken.

"What are you doing here?" he demanded, keeping his voice low. "Since when do women go to war?"

He heard her catch her breath and she replied angrily: "I come to help you though why I do not know."

Colorado, recovering from the surprise of seeing her, softened his voice. "I am happy to see you, Raven Wing. Always we were good friends."

"Snake Eye is still jealous," she said, accepting his attempt to conciliate her. "He knows I would prefer you." The sadness in her eyes did not show in the dark but the doleful tone of voice conveyed much to Colorado. It made him uncomfortable and he struggled for appropriate words.

"I am glad I have one loyal and true friend," he said eventually, feeling that even that was not good enough.

"How can I help you then?" she asked, aware of his discomfort and not wanting embarrassment between them.

Her words and offer of help moved Colorado and he wished he could have loved her. But he knew that in his past there had been nothing more than friendship for her. He felt angry at himself for his lack of deeper feeling.

"There is a way you could help, Raven Wing," he said, untying the heliograph Masterson had given him from around his neck and giving it to her.

She held it in her hand while he showed her how the shutter could be moved up and down so that the sun could be used to signal.

"Why do you give me this?" she asked when she understood the principle.

"When the sun rises, face east and move the shutter up and down so it captures the sun."

"The sun will not help you fight Snake Eye," she retorted, sounding puzzled.

"It will bring soldiers, girl! They ride in the east tomorrow." He rapped out the words with a trace of impatience, his conscience bothering him that he was asking her to act against her people. But there were other lives than his own involved in this and he couldn't afford too fine a conscience.

She considered for a moment then replied, "I will do it. But you must do your best to stop any killing of our poeple. It will be enough if you are safe."

"It will be as you say. Raven Wing will stay in my thoughts always."

He was embarrassed by his words. They seemed inappropriate against the risk she was taking for him. She sensed his feelings when she spoke.

"Go now, Colorado. Take care. May

the Gods of the mountains always protect you."

Wordlessly, he bent down and picked up the ram. When he had straightened he stared at her, the sadness in him again.

"I hope we may meet again," he said softly before turning away.

She watched him go down, back to the white eyes and when the darkness hid him, she wept.

16

THAT night on a low fire they cooked and greedily ate the bighorn. Any other time the meal would have been savoured, but this time, preoccupied with their danger and ravenous anyway, they ate quickly and mechanically, tearing at the meat with their fingers. It passed through each mind that maybe this was the last meal of the condemned.

The sun was rising slowly when they finished the last morsels. Colorado wiped the traces of juice from his mouth and took a swig of water to wash the food down. As he drank, a sudden chill premonition overcame him and he sensed, the way an animal senses, that the attack would come soon. Where from and how, he had no idea. Nothing was predictable about Apaches, especially one as petulant as Snake Eye.

When he inspected their defensive positions he was satisfied that they were well-placed to cover a frontal attack. The food they had eaten would boost morale for a while and substain them for at least another day. There was always the hope too, however forlorn, that if the attack did not come, Raven Wing might have attracted the bluecoats to the area. He had told the others that, thinking that some vestige of hope would help keep them going.

The first whoops and yells came when the sun burst into the fullness of its red glory. Peering intently beyond the defences, Colorado spotted heads popping up momentarily and then vanishing. Lithe bodies in crouching runs were scampering from rock to rock; the predators advancing towards their prey.

O'Hara saw them too and turned round. "When do we shoot?" he yelled, his trigger finger impatient and panic in his voice. "Can't see those red devils but for a second."

"Let 'em in close," Colorado shouted so everybody heard. "Close, where you can make sure."

As he finished the sentence, instinct made him turn towards the sheer rock face behind. It was in time to see the first Apache come bouncing backwards over the top ledge, the rope he was holding uncoiling and dangling below him. He kicked off the rock face again and again with his short powerful legs and the knife in his teeth glinted as a flash of sunlight caught it.

"So they're trying the back door too," Colorado thought.

Then another Mimbreno came over the ledge on another rope and others followed him. Like hungry, running spiders on gossamer strands, they descended, anxious to get to their prey.

Colorado called for some of the others to come to him and defend their rear. They spun round, confusion showing on their faces, believing the threat ahead too potent to be ignored.

Then, looking up, they saw the reason for his distraction for by now six Apaches were bouncing down the face, throwing their bodies out at wide angles to make shooting at them difficult.

The old-timer hurried to Colorado's side while the rest covered the front. Between the two defences, Liz and Diego held on to the spare rifles.

When the first Mimbreno hit the ground, he rolled and came to his feet, knife held high for his intended rush. Colorado saw the light of fanaticism in his eyes and the gruesome pale-blue warpaint on his cheeks. He waited calmly, his Winchester levelled, with the butt biting into his cheek and shoulder and then when the Apache was five yards away pumped a bullet into his throat tearing away the windpipe. Crimson blood spurted. The Apache staggered, fell, twitched convulsively and then was still.

The oldster shot another as he hit the ground and cursed as he was forced to reload. Colorado dropped to one knee and winged the next one before turning to check the others.

They were coping fine but when he spun again he was aware that the old-timer's rifle had jammed and he was struggling frantically with the ejection chamber. Looking ahead, he saw three Mimbrenos land and start sprinting. He shot two easily enough but the third came close and was only yards away when Colorado dropped him. Badly wounded, he dropped to his knees in a prayer-like attitude and held the pose as if he was about to perform a death chant. Colorado ignored him and devoted his attention to the other infiltrators still coming over the ledge. But it was a bad mistake. Using his last reserves of energy the Mimbreno forced himself to his feet and charged past the half-breed.

Colorado swung and pumped another shot into him but it was too late. With his last breath the Apache lunged at Liz and forced the knife between her shoulder blades. She gave a gasp and fell forward on to Diego knocking him over. The boy wriggled frantically from under his mother and desperately cradled her head, sobbing out his fear. Colorado watched the scene, horrified.

Then a blind rage took the boy and he wanted to hurt those who had hurt his mother. Demented in his fear and grief, he ignored Colorado's yells, and rushed at the Apaches. The nearest one took one swipe to stun him and then swept him up in his powerful arms. With his hostage the Mimbreno broke off to the right and sprinted for the rocks there, intending to work his way round the whites back to the main band. The other Apaches who had come down the rock face saw that they had a hostage and broke away too.

Colorado and the oldster joined the front defenders but after a few desultory exchanges the firing died away.

"They're gonna use the kid," Colorado said sadly.

"Sure are, son," the oldster replied.

When he was sure there would be no more action Colorado put his gun down and wearily plodded over to where Liz was lying. Star had moved her into the shadows, pulled out the knife and was cradling her head. The older woman looked up at Colorado and her eyes told him it was all up with the girl.

Colorado picked up a water bottle, bent down and poured some water onto Liz's lips. She opened her eyes briefly and smiled at him, filling him with an emptiness that was like a stabbing pain. The smile disappeared as she clutched his arm and moved her lips. But no words would come.

"She wants to tell you something," Star said, stating the obvious, her voice wavering in her grief.

Colorado bent down so that his ear was close to the girl's mouth. When he came up again, he smiled reassuringly and stroked her long golden hair. In return she forced a last smile but retracted it quickly, shutting her eyes as the last of the pain engulfed her. Colorado looked away from her dead eyes, futility gripping him like a cold hand; twice he had saved Liz only to see her die, as her husband had done, the victim of the Apaches, his own people. He figured there was no sense or pattern to it; the boy needed her more than ever now that he was fatherless.

"What did she say?" Star's voice seemed to be far away.

"She asked me . . . she asked me to take care of her boy."

"She thought a lot of you."

Colorado looked the woman in the eye. "I hope she's happy now," he stated flatly.

He walked away from the rest, fighting down his rage, while he looked out there to where his people held the boy. Suddenly he was all too well aware and ashamed of his blood.

"What'll happen?" The Lieutenant had come up beside him.

"They'll kill the boy."

"Just like that?"

Colorado's eyes turned on the soldier dismissively; he had no time for him, especially now. "Just like that," he repeated.

As if to confirm his assertion Snake Eye chose that moment to step out from cover holding the boy in front of him. In his free hand he was brandishing a tomahawk.

"You come out, all white eyes come out," he yelled, his threat to the boy requiring no statement.

"What'll we do?" the Lieutenant asked, beads of sweat standing out on his forehead. "We can't all go out there."

Colorado looked him up and down but there was no condemnation in the look, just a kind of pity and self-resignation. He knew what he had to do.

Studying the dishevelled group, he addressed Gant. "He only wants me. You and the others would be a bonus thrown in. You won't have to go out there." And then for the officer. "No sweat, Lieutenant."

"Snake Eye," Colorado's voice boomed before anybody could reply. "He who is uglier than the snake, answer me, Colorado."

"I hear you, white man. Speak with the tongue of the white man yet again."

"The boy goes free if I come," Colorado snarled. "But a man might be too much for you, traitor to your chief."

Snake Eye's laughing reply echoed round the canyon. "When we pull out your eyes white heart will not speak so boldly."

"You make woman's talk," Colorado replied, hiding his real fear. "Act instead of talking."

"When you are half-way to me I will let the boy go, Colorado. Walk swiftly to your fate."

Colorado cast aside his weapons and saw that the others were watching him. The woman opened her mouth to speak and Gant took a step towards him. But he didn't give them a chance to speak or interfere as he turned his back to them and stepped out. He shut them all out of his mind as he walked forward, steeling himself for what lay ahead, hoping he wouldn't let anyone see the fear that gripped his innards. He thought only of his promise to Liz and the life of the boy.

When he was well clear of cover, he saw Snake Eye smile and release Diego. Further back he spotted a movement as an Apache, armed with a bow and arrows, stepped from cover; evidently the boy didn't rate a bullet.

He kept his eyes firmly on the boy, who, apparently still affected from the blow he'd received, was traipsing towards him. As they met the boy grabbed Colorado's leg thankfully but the half-breed spun him round so that his own body protected the youngster from the Apache bowman.

A short sharp slap to the face gave him Diego's full attention.

"You've got to run and weave," he

said, "better than you've ever done."

Diego stared at him, coming out of his stupor, his eyes wide and frightened. "If you don't," Colorado went on, "one of them will kill you, understand?"

The boy nodded his head.

"Go now!" the half-breed commanded. "Live your life well."

Diego was going to speak but Colorado pushed him. His terror and his mentor's advice electrified the boy's legs and he shot off, running for his life. Colorado immediately faced the Mimbrenos, stepping into the bowman's line of flight to give the boy cover for as long as he could.

But eventually the Mimbreno released an arrow and Colorado heard it whistle as it passed close to him. He turned to see Diego stagger as it ripped into his shoulder. But the stumble was momentary and the youngster kept going. The second arrow clattered hopelessly against the rocks as he found sanctuary.

Colorado sighed. Probably the boy

would survive; it was a peripheral wound. The woman would know how to handle it.

He turned to his own problem and thought about running for it but doubted whether the Apache, who had strung another arrow, would miss him. Neither would the riflemen in the rocks, now the element of surprise had gone.

So he knew he'd have to go ahead, preserve life a little longer and hope for a miracle. Maybe he'd be able to endure some of their torture and maybe Raven Wing was already signalling for help. It was all he had left to hope for as he moved forward.

Snake Eye smiled his triumph when his enemy stood before him. Colorado held the Mimbreno's stare, refusing to drop his eyes, to admit any inferiority, and the insolence rattled the renegade so that he struck with the back of his hand. Colorado rolled his head back with the blow, tasted the blood on his lips and resumed his original position, forcing himself to smile.

Snake Eye called on two Apaches who came out of the rocks and took him by the arms. On their leader's orders they dragged him off into the rocks where other Mimbrenos had gathered. He took their scornful shouts without any reaction and did not struggle when they tied thongs to his arms and legs. Then they amused themselves pushing him from one to the other until their leader called a halt.

They dragged him out of the rocks to a piece of flat ground. As they drove the stake into the ground and tied him to it, he could smell his captors' foul breath. When they were finished that they stood back, staring at his spreadeagled form. One of them spat at him and the spittle ran down his cheek, adding to his humiliations. Yet throughout he remained oblivious to everything around him.

They left him there in the open, stretched out in the sun near the place where the two southerners had died;

left him to think. He knew that it had only just begun, that the merciless glare of the sun drilling into his eyeballs like sharp needles was a taste. Snake Eye would require more pain.

After an hour, when his lips were feeling dry, an Apache came out to him carrying a canteen. He got down on his knees near the half-breed and took the top off it. Colorado felt a sticky liquid running into his hair and down his cheeks. The smell of honey filled his nostrils and soon he could taste it in his mouth.

The Mimbreno grinned. "This will make you sweet, uh, son of the white woman."

Colorado watched him make a trail of honey leading away from where he lay and dribble the remnants over an ant hill. When he'd finished he came back and looked down quizzically at the half-breed.

"You bring soldiers," he said, pointing at the whites. "Now I bring an army to you. The ants will eat your eyes."

He went away sniggering, enjoying his joke, as Colorado turned his head to watch the first of the ants emerge and investigate their good fortune. He guessed it was all up with him now; the trail of honey marked his time. They would eat their way to him as surely as a lit fuse to dynamite, only it would be a slower fuse and at the end of it would be no sudden explosion but a greater and more drawn-out agony than imagination allowed.

He shut his eyes against the sun and sought calmness. Mainly he concentrated on the boy. When theants attacked him he'd keep the boy in his mind as the reason for this and he would see some purpose in his death.

Half an hour later he glanced along the honey trail and saw the ants were swarming over it now in a great horde. It was as if they were as anxious as Snake Eye and he began to hate them. When he turned away, fighting his fear, his mind involuntarily went back over his life and people he'd known and he let it roam; anything to escape thoughts of death crawling towards him. At one point Snake Eye's whining voice came to him.

"Are you afraid to watch your death as it comes to you," he taunted.

"Magnas will kill you one day," Colorado shouted.

"In one hand he will crush you."

Snake Eye's laughter was the only reply. The half breed shut his eyes, resenting the thongs which prevented him from being up and at his enemy.

The third time he looked Colorado felt his stomach muscles tighten with dread, for his small adversaries were only a foot away gorging themselves on the sweet honey. He twisted his neck in the opposite direction to increase the distance. Minutes seemed an eternity as he waited.

The sound of the gunshot surprised him and it crossed his mind that the whites were trying to kill him to spare him the pain. But on reflection it didn't make sense. They wouldn't be able to see the small ants at that distance, wouldn't know what he was facing. Then his mind registered more rifle fire coming from behind the Apaches' position.

He begun to hope and the cries and yells in Apache confirmed his optimism; the soldiers were attacking. He silently blessed Raven Wing and then desperately faced the ants again. They were so near now that he could see their small feelers working busily and he shuddered at the thought of what they could do to him.

Then he heard something off to the left and swung his head round to see Snake Eye coming towards him knife in hand, his face contorted with rage. Colorado was no longer concerned about the ants.

It was Gant's rifle which drove Snake Eye off, as two bullets kicked up the dust at the renegade's feet. Colorado watched him hesitate, think better of advancing and sprint away.

"Close one, that," Colorado heard a

voice say and looked up to see Gant standing over him, breathing heavily.

One kick of the white man's boot sent sand and ants in all directions. Colorado said a silent prayer as he saw the danger removed.

As Gant cut the thongs the half-breed stared at the rocks where Snake Eye had disappeared.

"I'll get him," he stated. "If it's the last thing I do."

"You betcha," Gant said, helping him up. The look on Colorado's face softened a little as he looked at the white man.

"Thanks," he said. Gant looked at his feet. "One I owe you, feller."

17

STAR was dressing Diego's wound when Colorado and Gant joined the others.

"He's okay," she said. "Thanks to you. He's passed out from the shock but he'll be all right."

The half-breed grunted his satisfaction and looked back at the rocks where the Mimbrenos had been. He saw them fleeing up the sides of the canyon, knowing that the soldiers, who were on horseback, would find following difficult.

He was glad for Raven Wing's sake that there had been no bloodshed so far, though if he could have laid his hands on Snake Eye he would have had no compunction about killing him. His eyes searched the slopes for his enemy and briefly caught a glimpse of him climbing high up. Star saw his edginess and frustration.

"Go after him! One day you'll have to anyway," she said, but Colorado making no reply studied Diego's prone figure. Star read his thoughts.

"Don't worry about him," she went on. "I'll look after him till you come back."

"He's not going anywhere," the Lieutenant said emphatically and when Colorado wheeled round he found himself facing the soldier's Colts.

Masterson's old arrogant composure was back and his self-doubt had disappeared now that they were being relieved.

Star's anger flared and the colour came to her cheeks.

"After all he's done," she screamed at the soldier, gesticulating wildly with her arms. "You're a crazy sonofabitch."

The others heard the confrontation too and gathered round. The old-timer spoke up. His voice was steady but underlined with menace.

"We'll all drop you, Lieutenant, if

you don't let him go. Ain't that right, fellers?"

The officer looked from face to face hoping for support but he found only implacable, silent agreement with the veteran's words.

"O'Hara, you'll back me!" Masterson said, his desperation making it sound more like a plea than an order.

O'Hara smiled slowly. "Can't rightly do that, sir. Lost my gun in action, sir!"

"Drop it, Masterson," Gant reiterated. "We're all agin you. That feller's a damn hero."

"You'll lose your stripes, O'Hara," Masterson tried his last ploy but it sounded weaker.

The sergeant looked at him derisively. "It'll be in a good cause then."

Without support, Masterson showed his true character, lowered his gun and stood to one side. Gant's eyes never left him.

"Go!" the woman repeated to Colorado, and when his eyes asked for reassurance, "I'll look after the kid."

"Thanks," he mumbled, looking to each in turn. Then he was off racing for the slopes.

He climbed with grim purpose, his body moving like an efficient machine that makes no unnecessary or wasteful movement. Relentlessly he ascended, ignoring the spray of bullets that the soldiers fired up at him believing him to be one of the renegades. Once, he looked down and saw the soldiers ride into the stronghold. Then he set his mind ahead and on Snake Eye.

His chest was heaving with effort when he reached the top and peered down at the vista below, where the land dropped quickly away into desert country. It was easy to pick out the fleeing Apaches and his keen eyes zeroed in on a figure he recognised as Snake Eye. He was far below, settling into a steady lope. Colorado found it strange that the Mimbrenos hadn't regrouped and could only think that they had agreed to make their way to a known rendezvous if they were split up. If that was it, then he would have a chance of catching Snake Eye alone.

Breathing easily again he set off down the slope keeping his eye on his enemy's direction though there wasn't much chance he would lose him; tracks in the desert made in a hurry were easy to read. It came down to a matter of time and stamina.

For an hour he gave chase. Occasionally the renegade would drop out of view down a sandy slope and be hidden by one of the rock clusters which chequered the flat land. Always, however, he would re-emerge and the distance between them narrowed to a half mile. Colorado spurred himself on anticipating the moment he would overtake Snake Eye.

It was this enthusiasm which made him, uncharacteristically, careless. Coming round some rocks he pulled up short and stared at the two horsemen who blocked his path a little way ahead. Comanches! Their bronze skins glistened in the sun and their long feathered lances lay across the ponies' necks as they appraised him. Unmistakably they were Comanches.

He froze and stuck out his chest, showing them that he was not afraid of the Apaches' hereditary enemies. Inwardly, however, he feared the odds; there were two of them, both mounted, and like all Comanches they would be expert horsemen. For the moment he forgot Snake Eye and wondered why he had stupidly left the Winchester behind.

The scorching heat and the desert silence, broken only by the snorting of an impatient horse, seemed portentous as Colorado slowly and deliberately drew his knife. Maybe if he was lucky they wouldn't fight. But they were hardly likely to ignore their good fortune when the odds were on their side.

He screwed up his eyes for closer inspection. One of the Comanches was youngish whilst the other seemed to be old for a warrior though his bearing suggested a veteran of many well-fought battles.

The older Comanche moved first, sliding easily off his pony. His eyes on Colorado, he bent down and untied his moccasins. The half-breed knew what the act signified; the Comanche was ashamed to have lived so long. Their tribe did not consider it manly to live too long for surely a true warrior would die young in battle. When the old Comanche removed his moccasins and put them to one side he was announcing that he would not run from that spot until he was dead or had killed his people's enemy; he was seeking death.

"You think maybe two Comanches cannot kill one Apache, huh?" Colorado hurled out his defiance when the warrior was back on his pony. "This is why you chose to seek death here, chicken heart?"

"We will come one at a time," the

young buck yelled back, his youthful pride hurt. "My uncle here will snuff out your life as easily as the wind blows the grass round our lodges."

"Let him come then and find death he seeks. It awaits him. There is much honour in dying at an Apache's hand."

It was enough. The veteran's full-bellied war cry rent the air as he dug his knees into his pony's flanks. Man and horse hurtled as one towards the half-breed, the drumming hooves mesmerising in the quietness around them. Colorado saw the long lance raised to shoulder height and held there as the Comanche's brown body hunched forward over the pony's neck. He braced himself knowing that the thrust would bear all the veteran's skill and only by waiting until the last moment would he match his adversary and avoid the probing metal death.

At two yards the horseman leant out and thrust forward with a quick smooth action. Colorado leant to one side, swaying sinuously at the hips and watching the ugly metal head of the spear pass inches from his chest. He grabbed for the wooden shaft, made it and felt the hot friction on his fingers as he held on for his life. His sudden pull and twist forced the horseman to release his own grip. As the Comanche fought to turn his horse to face Colorado, the half-breed leapt at him from behind and dragged him off.

They hit the ground in a swirl of dust, but Colorado wrestling free was first on his feet and to the lance. The Comanche was in a half-way sitting position when Colorado thrust the lance forwards and upwards into his gut. For long seconds he held that sitting position, staring at the wooden shaft of the lance, and a half-smile belying his agony as if he was savouring the welcome certainly of his honourable death. Then, without dignity, he flopped over and lay still, as lifeless and unbeknowing as the sand itself which one day would hide his bones and know nothing of his honour.

Colorado had no recovery time as the younger Comanche whooped his anger and started forward, his lance coming up and into the killing position. Colorado watched the taut muscles of the young brave's throwing arm as he pulled the war lance from the dead man's stomach. Fresh blood dripped from the metal point onto the yellow sand as he braced himself for the new onslaught.

He waited again for the lunge and this time went low under it so that the blade glanced off his back. When he came up, he was parallel with the horseman whose left side was exposed. Seizing the moment, as the pony swept past him he thrust his own lance upwards into the Comanche's side, twisted and let go. Then, breathing heavily, he watched man and horse continue the charge until fifteen yards away, of its own accord the pony pulled up, lowered its head and pawed at the ground directionless. On its back the Comanche sat unnaturally upright, like meat on a spit, as the lance protruded grotesquely at right angles to his body.

Then the weariness hit Colorado and he sank to his knees feeling the soreness running down his back where the lance had cut him. His eyes never left the Comanche who was still in that upright stiff position. Almost caressingly, the brave took the lance in both hands. Colorado heard the grunt as he pulled it out. For a time he thought the Comanche was going to turn and come at him again but instead he slid ponderously from his horse, staggered a few paces and then fell. Colorado felt the tautness leave his body with that fall.

The words and the voice, like a noose suddenly tightened, jerked at his nerves and brought a dry constriction to his throat. He spun round to trace their source.

Snake Eye, standing a couple of yards

away, had retrieved the Comanche's feathered lance and was laughing maniacally.

Heavy-limbed, Colorado forced himself to his feet and stood swaying, fatigued from his previous efforts. It was in his mind that if he had to die at least it would be facing his enemy.

"The Comanches are my friends today," Snake Eye exulted. "I will finish their work for them."

As the words trailed away, the half-breed lunged forward trying to grab the lance. The movement was clumsy and the Mimbreno stepped nimbly aside, allowing Colorado to lurch past him. He felt the shaft of the spear whip against his back as he stumbled and hit the dust.

When he turned over Snake Eye was standing astride him, lance poised. The leer on his face lingered as he enjoyed Colorado's humiliation and then his mouth tightened into vindictiveness as he remembered the past. Colorado knew he was about to strike to take his vengeance and there was little he could do about it except brace his body in natural preparation for pain.

But on the point of striking, Snake Eye's mouth suddenly unloosened and his eyes widened. Colorado, looking up, could not read the expression nor understand when his foe dropped the lance. Then the Mimbreno swayed, his legs buckled and he fell. His weight drove the air out of the half-breed as he landed on top of him.

Over the shoulder pressing against his throat Colorado saw the upright lance and then his fingers on Snake Eye's back felt the wet sticky blood as he pushed the Apache off him. The young Comanche was already flat out with the killing effort but raised his head out of the dust once to glare his hatred before he too died.

Colorado forced himself to his feet and watched the morose buzzards gather above in silent agreement, and hold back only because he was there and alive. It pleased him that when he moved off they would swoop down and devour his lifeless enemy until only his bones defiled the desert.

He walked stiffly to one of the ponies, threw himself onto it and headed in the general direction of the fort. Once he looked back but saw nothing but an empty sky.

18

AFTER resting the night, he reached the fort next day and spent the whole of it watching from the high ground, looking for the easy way in which would attract no attention. Around noon he spotted Star leave one of the adobe buildings to get some water from the well. She returned to the same building and he made a mental picture of it, for that would be where he would head, where the boy would be.

As darkness fell he worked his way in along the shallow ditch which led to the fort's extremities. The difficult part was the twenty-yards sprint from the ditch to the building but as he flattened against the nearest adobe he could detect no sign nor sound that his intrusion had been observed.

The rest was easy for one Apache-trained. The short crouching sprints, the quick search for the darkest corners, were as natural to him as eating and soon he was resting in the shadows of the adobe he had marked as Star's. The oil lamp was burning low when he looked through the window but he could make out Star's form sitting in an easy chair in the middle of the room. There was no one else around and that pleased him, though he was surprised they had given her such good quarters.

When he knocked on the door Star's voice inquired who was there.

She didn't hear his first low whispering of his name but the second time the low light went out and there was a hurried unbarring of the door.

"Thank God you made it," she exclaimed as he stepped inside.

"They looking for me?" he asked.

Star sighed. "Masterson made it bad for you. All the others did their best but he's the soldier and his words carry most weight."

"Thought that would be the way of it."

She turned the lamp on low and pulled the curtains, gesturing for him to sit down. He sank into the chair and it felt good to him after the rigours of the trail but he didn't allow the comfort to divert him from his real reason for being there.

"How's the boy?" he asked, taking the cup of coffee she had poured for him.

"Fine," she retorted. "A little bit sad most of the time but what would you expect. I've done my best to reassure him that things would be okay."

"I'm grateful, ma'am. He needed somebody to look after him."

"You looked after us, didn't you," she replied. "We'd be dead otherwise."

"I'll take him to my ma and pa," he went on. "They'll look after him till he's of age to make his own way. They know how things are for a half-breed."

"The way they are for you?" There

was a hint of sympathy in the voice.

"That's right, ma'am," he replied. "Takes one to know."

"I'll bring Diego to you in the morning. We'll meet you out in the hills where it'll be safe."

"That's a good idea, ma'am. Right now I'd like to sleep for a couple of hours if that's okay?"

She nodded her assent. "I'll wake you in two hours."

Sleep came easily to him. In that cabin for the first time for days he felt safe even though all around were soldiers. The tension of the trail and battle slid away as the gentle light seduced his heavy eyes and the soft chair accommodated his heavy, wearied limbs. His dreams were peaceful too until one of them was interrupted by an incongruous staccato rapping. In his somnolent state it seemed distant, irrelevant, until it persisted and became more real than the dream he slipped out of into a still drowsy half-wakened state.

The woman shook him. He woke completely then and the rapping boomed insolently into the silence.

"They must know you're here," the woman said anxiously as he pushed out of the chair.

"There's no other way out?" he asked, looking around.

She shook her head negatively, despairingly.

"Try and bluff it," he said, stepping back into the shadows. "Maybe they don't know."

But as soon as she had lifted the bar somebody's boot kicked the door open. She started back as two figures hurtled into the room, paused fractionally, and then trained rifles on Colorado. The half-breed looked beyond the barrels, saw Masterson's pompous face, then focused on Bill Tidy's twisted jaw and hatred filled his eyes.

"I'm only one half-injun and unarmed," he said, mocking them. "Two rifles for one half-breed, huh?"

"Thanks for the information, Mr

Tidy," Masterson said, ignoring Colorado.

"My pleasure. Just so long as the army jail him for about twenty years or hang him," Tidy replied, his mocking, malevolent eyes never leaving Colorado's face.

"He'll be taken care of," Masterson said, gloating but staring away from Colorado into the corner of the room as if he was reluctant to meet the half-breed's eyes.

"You're a rat, Masterson," Star shrieked almost hysterically. "The lowest stinking rat in the goddam sewer."

The officer blushed but gave her no reply.

"Outside!" he snapped at Colorado, jerking his rifle in that direction.

Colorado complied and Tidy followed them out into the moonlight.

"Cowards! Gutter trash!" Star called after them, venting her frustration.

Colorado felt Tidy's rifle jab into his spine and he winced.

"Jail's straight ahead a mite," he snapped. Then more softly, almost conversationally, "But run if you want to."

Colorado started walking towards the jail. Once before, he remembered, he'd been taken there. But General Crook had got him out. He didn't figure Crook could help him this time.

"Figured you for a backshooter," he said to Tidy half-way across the parade ground. "Didn't think you'd hand me over to the army."

"Nothing I'd like better than to backshoot you, injun. But this way I get reward money too and the army'll do the business for me. Ain't that right, Lieutenant?"

"You'll get your money, Tidy," Masterson replied. "And he'll get what all deserters get."

The brief glimpse of his cell that the light of the hurricane lamp gave him before his captors took it away, told him that it was just as it had been. He reflected as he lay in the darkness that nothing much had changed for him since he'd last been shut away.

He'd had a few adventures and now quite probably he'd rot for a long time in a white man's jail; that was if they didn't hang him. His fate had been diverted for a while that was all.

Next day he felt rested, refreshed. Star twice brought him food but the visits were fleeting. She tried to comfort him and reassure him that things would work out but he didn't need her to. Philosophically he had already accepted his situation.

Next night the sound of low voices woke him. He sat up just as the two corporals who had been guarding him were bundled through the door that led to the cells. The figure behind who had the rope draped over his shoulder and was holding the gun, pushed their bodies against the bars of Colorado's cell and peered over their shoulders. Colorado recognised Gant even though he wore a bandana over the lower half of his face.

Then the keys to the cells clattered at

Colorado's feet where Gant had thrown them and he stooped unhurriedly to pick them up.

"You're sure not as anxious as me to get the hell out of here," Gant said reprovingly as Colorado took his time trying the keys in the lock.

When he was out, they pushed the jailers into the cell. Gant locked it and took the keys with him into the outer office.

"I'm grateful to you, mister," Colorado said, following him. He picked up one of the corporals' rifles and checked the breech.

"Star told me what had happened," Gant replied. "You've got to get out of here fast."

"I'm taking the boy with me," Colorado answered.

Gant's eyes registered surprise. "It'll be dangerous to hang around. There's men after you, and Johnson's here. Saw him ride in today."

Colorado studied Gant accusingly. "How do you know Johnson?"

Gant lowered his bandana as if it would obscure the truth, make his confession sacrilegious. "I'm a bounty hunter. I was headed for the fort when the stagecoach was attacked. I was coming to look for you."

Colorado studied him, showing no emotion. "How much?"

"Fifty thousand dead or alive."

"Tom Gordon wants me badly then," Colorado mused.

"Pretty bad. He was a proud father."

"You don't aim to collect?"

Gant sighed and looked away from Colorado, his eyes taking on a dreamy look, his memory transporting him across the years.

"I was decent once," he said, "and out there you started to remind me. I couldn't kill you after what happened."

Colorado nodded. "Let's get the boy. He's at Star's place."

Star was ready for them and quickly let them in when Colorado knocked on the door.

"I thought you might come for the

boy," she said, disappearing into the bedroom.

Diego came out with her, pulling on his shirt. When he saw Colorado his face lit up into a big smile.

"You're coming with me, amigo," the half-breed told him. "Say goodbye to Star."

While the boy and woman embraced, Colorado shook Gant's hand.

"There's two horses round the back," Gant told him. "But watch your backtrail, uh?"

Colorado smiled faintly. "Always been watching my backtrail."

When the half-breed and the boy were mounted, hurried goodbyes were said and then they kicked the horses into action. In the distance, at the fort's extremities, there were some shouts and commotion as the guards heard the horses' drumming hooves but there was no gunfire. Colorado and the boy were clear, riding off across the desert.

19

LOOKING down on Brannigan's place, Colorado saw his stepfather chopping wood. His mother was tending the small garden at one end of the cabin. The domestic scene carried an aura of peace and not for the first time Colorado appreciated the fact that his mother had met a man like Brannigan.

"That's your new home," he told Diego as they spurred down the narrow valley to the cabin. "See those horses in the corral? Brannigan will teach you how to ride 'em and maybe give you one for yourself."

Diego smiled. "He is your father, huh?"

"No but he's as good as. He's as straight as an arrow and not bothered about the colour of a feller's skin. It's what's inside the skin that counts with him."

Colorado's mother straightened her back and put down the hoe as she saw them coming. One hand shaded her eyes from the sun as she studied them more closely. Then when she recognised the tall one she began running.

Colorado reined in and leapt off his horse to meet her embrace. His strong arms lifted her off the ground and when he put her down he saw the tears in her eyes.

"It's good to see you, son," she understated and courteously turned to the boy, "and your friend."

"This here's Diego. His ma and pa were killed by the Mimbrenos so I've brought him to you."

"You're welcome, boy," she said, her eyes smiling at Diego. "Right now you two could do with a meal I guess."

They followed her on foot, leading the horses. Brannigan met them halfway and embraced Colorado.

"Good to see you," the big white man said, standing back and looking his step-son up and down. Then his eyes drifted off into the mid-distance and Colorado knew that he was concerned that they weren't followed.

"It's all right for awhile," he said softly so his mother wouldn't hear.

Inside the cabin they tucked into platefuls of stew. Diego quickly felt at ease and chatted away. Brannigan wisely talked about things of interest to a boy his age, avoiding questions about his mother and father. Colorado sensed that Diego would have no trouble settling in. He thought about Liz and a feeling of sadness swept over him; that the boy should be left without his ma troubled his sense of justice. But he knew there was little justice in the world. Soon the bounty hunters would be hot on his own trail and they would kill him for money regardless of his innocence.

"Are they still after you?" Brannigan asked as if reading his stepson's thoughts.

"I bust out of jail," Colorado replied. "Did nothing wrong to be there, ma.

Did what was right."

Brannigan's bushy eyebrows lowered into a frown. "So tonight you'll be safe?"

Colorado nodded. "I hid the trail well and got a good start."

"You'll be going again tomorrow?" his mother asked, looking disappointed.

"Tomorrow I'll head for Mexico and cross the border. Should have done that before."

"Whatever you think," she replied, and Colorado knew she was asserting her stoicism to overcome her emotions.

The rest of the evening was spent in pleasant conversation and when darkness fell Diego was sent off to bed. Then Colorado spent another hour reminiscing with Brannigan and his ma. The love he felt for them both would make it difficult to leave in the morning. He knew that the family feeling was rare and was glad that Diego would share it. For himself, it saddened him that it might be a long time before he rode back again. Out there, in the night, was a colder world than here amongst those closest to him.

It was late when the talk died and Brannigan finally blew out the lamp. Colorado, unused to a bed, stayed in the kitchen and settled down on the floor.

Meanwhile, out there in the desert, the cold descended on one white man and his two Apaches as they bedded down. Bill Tidy cursed the cold and wished he could build a fire. But having got that close to the man he hated, he wasn't going to give their position away. The Apaches he'd hired had done a good job getting him to within easy reach of Brannigan's place. He figured they'd wait for light, watch the cabin and choose their moment. He rubbed his jaw where the cold had got at it and remembered Colorado's rifle butt.

20

WHEN the sun came up, Colorado rose with it and collected his things. His mother, understanding his need to be on the move, helped him and then cooked him a good breakfast.

When he'd eaten she went to waken Diego but Colorado stopped her.

"I've said too many goodbyes recently, ma. The kid would be better left sleeping."

Brannigan brought him his horse and he mounted up.

"I'll be thinking of you," he said to them both before kicking it into action.

On the hill above the cabin, the Apache shook Bill Tidy awake and pointed to the solitary rider. The white man leapt out of his blankets, picked up his field-glasses and studied the figure. Looking through the lenses, he felt he could almost reach out and touch Colorado and he was enervated.

"It's him. Let's get going," he shouted, and rushed to saddle his horse.

The Apaches followed him down the slope. One of them had to tell him to slow up or they'd be seen.

They hung well back reading Colorado's sign. Eventually one of the Apaches pin-pointed his direction.

"He heads for the Rio Grande," he told Tidy.

The white man frowned. "We'll have to close up soon, take him this side of the river before he crosses the border."

They speeded up, driving their tired horses. But up ahead, Colorado already knew they were coming. He had stopped for a while to watch his back trail and had seen the three horsemen, two of them obviously Apache trackers. From then on he used all his tricks and now and then stopped to watch their attempts to unravel the mysteries he was creating. He knew he was good enough to out-think them and make the border crossing.

21

WHEN he sighted the familiar river it brought back memories, for during their raids the Mimbrenos had crossed and recrossed the stretch he was looking at now. It wasn't far ahead; he estimated two miles across flat land. His pursuers were still well back and he was confident that once in Mexico he'd be safe from the cavalry, and those three behind, whoever they were, would be easy to lose.

He rode easily for half a mile and then stopped to drink from his canteen, but as he recorked he heard a horse snort, somewhere off to his left. Dismounting quickly, he led his horse behind some pinon trees and waited, his eyes scouring the scattered trees and brush.

He knew that his three followers

couldn't have got in front and didn't expect any bounty hunter to be up ahead of him. He presumed the noise would be from an innocent party of riders but it would be wise and sensible to hide until they had passed.

The party eventually emerged from a cluster of trees to his left. Its members were moving slowly and making dust so he had to strain to identify features. But he heard a whip crack several times before the picture became clear. When it did clarify he had a sick feeling in his stomach and old hostilities revived.

Four white men rode guard on two Apaches who were dragged, half-staggering, behind the horses. The white men were laughing and poking fun at their captives and the one dressed in black who carried the whip would flay an Apache every time he stumbled or slowed up. Colorado, watching from the trees, winced each time the lash made contact.

He knew the whites were slave traders who were taking the Apaches across the border where they would sell them to some rich mine owner who would work them to death. He had heard many tales of the cruel conditions in the mine from Mimbrenos who had escaped the horror.

When the party came level with him and about fifteen yards off he could see the ugly weals on the Apaches, on their backs where the gringo in the black hat had done his work. The scars on Magnas's back flashed into his mind and he knew what he had to do.

He rode casually out of the trees, drawing his pistol and made a straight line towards the traders. There was no rush about him, just a grim certainty of purpose.

None of the whites saw him at first, being too preoccupied with taunting their captives. Then Black Hat suddenly glanced in his direction. His mocking smile vanished and he dropped the whip shouting to the others.

As they reached for their rifles Colorado dropped low over the neck of the horse and kicked hard, aiming his pistol. He had time to see the panic on their faces and the frantic pulling of rifles from their scabbards before he unleashed his first shot. It took Black Hat in the mouth and exited through the cheek. The man fell from his horse screaming his pain.

As he broke their ranks, he aimed again and gutshot another of the whites. The man grasped at his stomach with both hands as his entrails came pouring out like meat minced.

His dash took him clear and he pulled his horse round again ready for a second charge. But the two Apaches had not been idle. The other whites had been knocked off their horses and killed with their own knives. Black Hat had been knifed to finish him off. When Colorado approached, they were already scalping.

"Thank you, nephew of Magnas," one of them said when they both stood up. "We have seen you with your uncle many times."

"We are Mescalero," the other added. "You will always be welcome in our camp after what you have done."

Colorado nodded. "Right now I must leave," he said, pulling his horse's head round so it faced in the direction of the river. "One day I may seek your hospitality."

He left them there and rode for the border. He knew he had still a mile and a half to go and he could not be sure exactly how long the fracas had delayed him. It half-worried him that whoever was behind could have closed up considerably and the thought made him urge his horse into a fast canter.

After a mile, the trees disappeared giving way to cacti. He rode through them unconcernedly, not considering any of them good enough cover for a man, and when he rode out of them, the blue ribbon of the Rio Grande was a hundred yards off across perfectly flat land. His eyes picked out a place where the river was calm and easy to cross and he headed for it.

At the river he stopped and looked round but nobody was following so he let his horse drink before prompting it into the water. The cool water against his moccasins was refreshing after his hard ride. Ahead lay Mexico and relief from the chase. He began to dream of tequila and lazy days in the sun. Perhaps some senorita might take a fancy to a half-breed who looked . . .

"Crack!" Like an ogre into a peaceful dream the gunshot blasted into his fantasies and he felt his horse stumble, struggle to recover and then crash down into the shallow water. He tried to dive clear but he had relaxed too much and it made the difference. He felt the water, like grasping fingers, on his face, kept his head up and pulled at his legs. The right one came free but the left, with the full weight of the horse on it, was immovable. Giving up the struggle he reached for the scabbard on the saddle, and gripped the stock of his rifle. But he was never to pull it clear. A searing pain shot through his spine as the rifle butt came down between his shoulder blades.

In agony he twisted his body and looked back to the bank behind him. The two Apache trackers showed no emotion as they held their guns on him. Their wet clothes told the story; they had been given time to get ahead and conceal themselves in the water. He figured this time he would not escape.

Seconds later Tidy rode up in a rush and jumped off his horse.

"Never took you for a complete idiot," he said laughing. "You could have been clear away if'n you hadn't stopped back there. But we are mighty grateful to you, aren't we, boys?"

"We get lots of money, huh?" one of the Apaches asked smiling.

"Sure will, boys," Tidy confirmed. "But I have a little matter to settle with him."

He reached for his lariat, uncoiled it and swung it cow fashion. When he released it the noose landed over Colorado's shoulders. Then the white man walked into the water and adjusted it until it was under the half-breed's arm-pits. He tied the other end to the pommel of his horse. It was all done in silence.

"Now comes the fun," he shouted while the trackers went off to get their horses.

When the Apaches were ready he kicked his horse's flanks. The pain in Colorado's leg, as he was dragged clear of his own horse, almost made him faint.

Tidy cantered at first while behind the dust filled Colorado's nose and mouth so that he strove for breath. He felt every bone in his body as he was dragged over the worst undulations.

But the real torture came when they reached the cacti. Instead of riding straight through Tidy speeded up and criss-crossed so that Colorado was flung against the plants. Each time he hit one, fresh areas of pain were opened up so when they emerged into the trees he was badly bruised and bleeding. Once when he was twisted onto his back he looked down and saw through glazed eyes his bloodied body. It was only when he became semi-conscious that they loaded him onto the spare packhorse like a sack.

Curious eyes turned on them as they rode in. Colorado's body slumped across the horse made them inquisitive. But few recognised the half-breed.

Tidy dismounted outside Masterson's office, dismissed the trackers, dragged the body off the bronc and let it fall untidily into the dust. The officer came out on to the boardwalk.

"There he is, Lieutenant," Tidy announced, putting his toe to the body. "He'll never bring grief to anybody again." He bent over and tore the necklace from Colorado's neck.

"This'll do for a trophy," he said, putting it round his own neck.

Masterson inspected the bloodied body and smiled at Tidy. The smile was the relieved kind, the type a person gives when he feels a source of embarrassment will soon be removed.

"Tom Gordon will wire you the reward," Masterson told him, "after Johnson has positively identified him."

"That's the injun all right, as me and you know, Lieutenant," Tidy said superfluously as he turned his horse.

"Anyone wants me I'll be in the sutler's."

22

TIDY leaned against the bar in the sutler's and knocked back the whisky. He smiled superciliously and in a mood of self-satisfaction raised his next glass to his own reflection in the mirror.

"Well done, Bill," a soldier congratulated him.

"The bastard paid, eh?" Tidy said, louder than he had to so that others in the room could hear.

"Nobody messes me about."

"There'll soon be one less coon in the world anyhow," someone in the corner said and others agreed.

"Drinks all round, boys," Tidy shouted, turning and gesturing expansively. "I've got some money coming to me."

There was a rush to the bar where a multitude of grasping hands seized the glasses as soon as the bartender had poured. Toasts were drunk to Tidy's success, bolstering his pride.

The drink flowed, sparked by Tidy's initial enthusiasm and the talk became louder.

"Looking for you, Tidy!" An ice-cool, melancholy voice, incongruous amongst the merriment, suddenly brought silence to the crowd.

Gant stood in the doorway and all eyes turned to him.

"Why you lookin'," Tidy said, drawing himself to his full height as a path cleared between them.

"Gonna kill you."

Tidy's eyebrows came down in an aggressive frown and his eyes widened.

"You can try anytime, mister," he replied. "But I always prefer knowing why the man I face wants to die."

Gant jerked his thumb over his shoulder. "The feller you brought in."

Tidy smiled. "That was all legal, mister. The army wanted him."

"If you'd faced him like a man, I wouldn't be here," Gant said. "Instead, he's like a piece of raw meat."

Tidy shrugged. "He's part injun, ain't he? There's free range on wild ones."

Gant's right hand dropped to his gun. "Time you stopped talking and made your move before I do."

Tidy's features set hard. "Okay, mister, if you want to die 'cos of one lousy injun . . ."

As his words tailed off he went for his gun. It was a fast draw but Gant was quicker and Tidy's gun was just levelling when the bullet ripped into his forehead. His whole body went stiff and his arms stretched out in front of him as the blood oozed from his wound onto his face. With a pained look and wide-eyed amazement, he studied Gant. The latter put another bullet into his chest and he fell forward crashing onto the floor. His gun skidded across the smooth floor into a crowd of onlookers. Gant stood over the body and then bent down and ripped Colorado's necklace from Tidy's neck.

"This don't belong to him," he said to the hushed onlookers. "And he ain't fit to wear it."

He backed towards the door, covering the crowd with his gun. Once outside, he rushed to his horse, mounted it and sent it into a gallop, heading towards the desert.

A few miles out he halted and looked back but nobody was following. He leant forward and gently stroked his horse's nose.

"One more thing to do," he said to himself and eased the animal into a steady canter.

23

TWO days later Colorado opened his eyes and gradually the fog in his mind lifted. The bed was warm and luxurious but the pain in his body still tormented him. Peering round, he realised that he was in a rough and ready sick bay. The whitewashed walls and cleanliness of the room suggested it.

Slowly the events of the last week came back to him and, as he remembered how close he had been to the border and anonymity in Mexico, a cynical smile twisted his lips. Outside, he saw soldiers moving about and figured Tidy must have brought him back to the fort. It seemed to him a kind of destiny that he should return there. It seemed too that he would never get away from it.

In the ensuing days, Star came to visit him often. She was full of talk and plans to escape but he knew none of them was workable. However he appreciated her kindness and when O'Hara came to visit him a couple of times he appreciated that too. It was good to have white folk acting friendly towards him.

However, there was an unwelcome visitor as well. On the third day of his confinement, the door of the hospital burst open and a tall, craggy-faced, ageing man stepped in, his gnarled fists bunched at his sides. The private who was escorting him looked abashed, probably surmising that the man in his charge was uncontrollable.

Narrow intense eyes looked down on Colorado out of that craggy face which suffused a lethal combination of torment and hate. The malevolent energy belied the man's age, making him seem much younger.

"Come to see the skunk who killed my son," a gravelly voice bellowed.

Colorado knew then that he was Tom Gordon. He knew, too, there was no placating the man; those eyes drilling into him made that clear. He recognised and understood that kind of hate well. When he had killed the man's son it had been hate riding him, spurring into him. That kind of feeling had to have an outlet or turn inwards, biting at a man's innards. Tom Gordon, for certain, was feeling its compulsion.

"You're gonna die, injun," he said with deadly intensity. "They say you'll die in front of a firing squad but if I get to you first there's no telling how it will be." He drew his hand across wet lips. "Think on that while you lie there. Think how a man's son is his most precious possession and how you took mine away from me."

The bitter memory brought a purple flush to Gordon's cheeks. The private stepped forward and hesitantly thrust his rifle between Colorado and his tormentor. But Gordon contained himself and spun on his heel, making for the door where he paused and looked back.

"They say Hell's hot, mister," was his parting shot.

Colorado dismissed the words and the incident. There wasn't much anyone could do to him while he was a guest of the United States Army.

24

THE days passed untroubled and the time came when he could leave his bed and walk tentatively round the room. His progress had been reported for it was not long after that he was sent for. Two youngish soldiers formed the escort for the prisoner as he was urged across the now familiar parade ground to General Crook's headquarters.

"They're gonna try you today," one of the soldiers said as if he was reporting on the weather. "Just thought I'd tell you."

Crook looked up from his seat at the big table as Colorado's guards came to attention. At a nod of his head they stepped back. The officers seated on either side of the General studied the prisoner and the majority of them felt it an impertinence that he held each one's stare, his eyes roving from one to another as if in challenge. Most of them looked away first. To his left and seated, Colorado saw Sergeant O'Hara and Lieutenant Masterson, friend and foe together.

General Crook began without preliminaries.

"You were one of the scouts led by Scar and attached to Lieutenant Masterson when our troops attacked the camp of the Apache known as Chunte? Is that correct?"

"That is true, General."

"On that occasion," Crook went on, "did you mutiny, turning your rifle on soldiers of the United States Cavalry, and did you furthermore desert?"

"It is true what you have said," Colorado replied evenly.

Crook leaned back, studying the half-breed, remembering their first meeting when he had been impressed.

"You know the consequence of those actions?" he asked quizzically.

"Probably you'll shoot me?"

"Well!" Crook expelled a big breath. "If you're admitting this calamity there's only one way it can end. What can you say in your own defence?"

Colorado turned slowly in Masterson's direction and he studied the Lieutenant disdainfully.

"That man wanted glory," he said quietly. "He never gave the Tontos a chance. When they did give up and laid down their weapons he shot them. He has no honour, that one."

Masterson, at these words, shifted uncomfortably in his chair and kept his eyes lowered. A pregnant silence followed. It was broken by the scraping of chairs as some of the officers sat forward, more interested now. At last Crook's eyes swivelled towards the Lieutenant.

"What do you say?"

Masterson looked up, forced his eyes to meet the General's and cleared his throat.

"Sir, they came down the trail at us. That's all I know."

"Did they surrender, Lieutenant?" Crook persisted.

"Sir, I . . . " O'Hara interrupted, but a rebuking glare from the General quietened him.

Masterson, feeling the power of all eyes on him like physical blows, played nervously with the headband of his hat.

"They didn't surrender, sir," he said finally. "I saw those savages coming down the trail and I knew it was my job to kill them."

Crook turned back to Colorado, hoping Masterson's words were true as he believed a brother officer's should be.

"They were unarmed when he cut them down," the half-breed reiterated in a wearied, bored voice.

"Sergeant O'Hara. You were there. What's your story?" Crook rasped.

O'Hara climbed out of his chair and stood at ease, his big jaw jutting with determination, to say his piece and vindicate Colorado.

"I was there, sir, and I'm pretty ashamed admitting it, sir," he began. "Sure enough Colorado held me and my men at rifle point and called the Tontos out. They came out just as he said, sir, and unarmed. That's when the Lieutenant shot them down."

Crook visibly winced. "You're agreeing with the accused?"

"Yes, sir. Later he saved my life and some others too, including the Lieutenant's."

There was a silence in the room and the officers were totally absorbed now. It was rare that a sergeant would disagree so blatantly with his officer. O'Hara was an old sweat, not far off his pension. He had a great deal to lose.

Crook stroked his chin absentmindedly, thanked O'Hara and then turned to his officers.

"I think, gentlemen, that this needs some careful discussion."

Along the table heads nodded in agreement.

The General addressed Colorado.

"We will recall you when we've talked. Meanwhile you and the witnesses can wait in my outer office."

The argument began as soon as they left the room. Some of the officers tended to believe there might be truth in O'Hara's version of events but others, more naïve, were unwilling to believe one of their own kind would bring dishonour to them. Yet, in the end, deeper than their divisions ran the feeling that they must protect their own status. If Masterson lost credibility, if the story came out, then it would affect all officers, for morale amongst those in the ranks would suffer.

Crook tried to be fair but their feelings overrode his attempts at impartiality too. In the end, the salve to their collective conscience was that though Colorado might just have a case, he had deserted; that was the straw they clutched when the majority found him guilty.

Colorado knew when he was brought back into the room; he could smell his own death. Crook stopped playing with his tunic button and studied the half-breed. He saw something in Colorado's bearing, a contained, dignified self-possession which gave the lie to the accusation that this man would desert wilfully. His soldier's eye made a full appraisal and his voice was low, regretful, when he pronounced the verdict.

"Colorado. This board finds some doubt about the surrender business. It can't be proved either way — seems one man's word against another's."

The relieved sigh emanating from O'Hara was stifled by a severe look from the General.

"However, be that as it may you still raised a rifle against cavalrymen whilst on attached duty and duly forsworn to protect them. Then, worse, you committed the crime most heinous to all members of this army — you deserted." He continued: "On the grounds of your mutiny and desertion I hereby sentence you to death by firing squad one week from this day."

Crook rushed the last punishing words and then rustled the papers in front of him as if that would forestall the awesome silence which habitually followed such a sentence. In those moments, as he reflected on his own words, he felt acutely his own mortality. It was as if a jester sat on his shoulder, mocking his judicial pretensions. The doubt involved in this case made him more sensitive to the feeling.

Colorado stone-facedly turned his eyes towards Masterson and then O'Hara. He noticed the frown creasing the sergeant's brow. Then the big man leapt to his feet kicking over his chair. Masterson cowered back.

"What are you doing, O'Hara?" Crook demanded.

"Getting rid of the dirt clinging to my arms," O'Hara bellowed back as he ripped off the yellow stripes from his arm.

The two soldiers at the door stepped forward and looked to the General, half-reluctantly waiting the order to arrest O'Hara and fearing his size and power.

"Don't worry, I'll arrest myself, General," O'Hara announced, stepping towards them and placing himself between them.

"Used to respect this army. Been my home for twenty years. But now this dirt will always cling to me and you've done it." His eyes roved along the line of officers.

"Take me away, boys, and I'll wipe your noses for you."

He finished speaking, did an about-turn and quick-marched out of the door, the two soldiers stumbling untidily after him.

Minutes later Colorado followed, back to the cells, with just seven suns left to live.

25

COLORADO watched O'Hara with curiosity. Nothing but bars divided them now for they had been put in adjacent cells. He could tell from the big man's demeanour that he was still seething.

"Can't figure you," he stated, leaning against the bars, eyeing the erstwhile enemy who had sacrificed his career for a principle, for his sake.

"How's that?" O'Hara asked, some of his normal control returning.

"You've changed. Can't figure men who change."

O'Hara narrowed his eyes and spoke quietly as if to himself.

"Hate!"

Colorado nodded slowly. "That I do understand."

He invited no explanation but the sergeant began one.

"Twenty years ago," he mused, looking upwards into space, his eyes searching, lifting the veil of the years.

"Twenty years ago I rode down into Arizona, back home after some hell raisin'. I found my ma and pa dead. White Mountain 'pache did it. It was a hell of a sight." He turned his eyes back to Colorado.

Colorado speculated, "So you joined the Army to fight Apache?"

"That's why I joined, that's what I've been doing," O'Hara replied. "Guess I've always hated myself too for not being back home when those 'paches came down on them. Instead I was riding with a wild bunch."

"What will they do to you now?" asked Colorado.

O'Hara smiled carelessly. "Lose my pension, not much more."

"I'm sorry."

"Could have lost my life a week or two back. What's a pension."

"What'll you do when you leave here?" Colorado asked, thinking that was one question which would never again apply to himself.

"Help a friend to run a horse ranch — back in Arizona. I've got some money stashed."

"Good work-horses. You're lucky."

O'Hara nodded. "Let's hope we both get luck, especially you," he said and lay down on his bunk.

In moments he was asleep and snoring resonantly. The sun, going down, cast long shadows across the cell floor as Colorado lay down too.

It was when the sun died and the fort had gone quiet, except for a few night sounds, that the door of the cell crashed open and a hurricane lamp cast its yellow light on the two reclining figures. Instinctively Colorado sat up and peered.

"That's him," snapped a disembodied voice from somewhere behind the light.

Then there was movement and three men loomed and took more distinct shape as they pressed against the bars. Three grim faces huddled close and stared at him from behind the lamp, like primitive men behind a flickering fire, their eyes inhuman, hollowed sockets in the shadowy light. One of them turned the lamp up.

Tom Gordon's face animated with excitement as the extra light confirmed that it was indeed his son's killer. He fingered the bull whip lasciviously.

"The keys. The keys, man!" he rapped impatiently to one of the lumbering cowboys at his side.

The man unlocked the door and the old rancher kicked it open in his haste. As he entered, he drew and cocked his forty-five.

Colorado watched impassively, figuring death might be coming earlier to him than the U.S. Cavalry anticipated. He saw O'Hara sit up on his bunk and in the same instant one of the cowboys turned and trained his rifle on the sergeant.

"Tie him up good," Gordon told the cowboy who was carrying the rope.

At the point of a gun Colorado

had to submit. When his arms were tied behind him he was pulled to his feet and bundled forward. While he was being tied face-first against the bars, Gordon kicked him viciously behind the knees and uncoiled the bull whip.

"This is going to be for me," he said, pressing his face so close to Colorado's that the half-breed could smell his breath. "The Army's gonna shoot you but that's too quick for my liking. This is for my pain which won't never go away."

Colorado looked grimly ahead, steadying himself as the old rancher prepared to strike.

The first blow seared through his shirt as neatly as a knife through butter and his back muscles tightened involuntarily. Gordon snorted his triumph, moved sideways and drew back the lash for a second time. The two cowboys watched fascinated, distracted by the primitive ritual, by the red line of blood bubbling through

Colorado's broken skin and onto his shirt.

But Gordon didn't make the second strike, for an arm snaking through the bars aborted it, gripping the lash and jerking backwards. Gordon balanced and toppled. Before he drew another breath, both O'Hara's arms shot out and encircled the old man's neck. All the air exited from his lungs and a hard lump constricted his windpipe as he was reeled in. Momentarily, one of the sergeant's arms dropped to Gordon's holster and pulled the forty-five. Then it was up again, pointing the gun at the two dumb-struck cowboys.

"Drop your rifles and untie your gunbelts, fellers," O'Hara ordered, bringing back the hammer of the gun. "Untie him."

The two men exchanged glances and in mutual agreement did as they were told. Colorado felt the blood draining back into his hands as they unloosened his bonds. He grabbed one of the fallen rifles like a drowning man grasping a lifeline and held it caressingly. The cowboys backed voluntarily against the bars and he read fear in their eyes at the sudden reversal of fortune. O'Hara released the old man who slumped to the floor where he lay writhing and fighting for breath.

The sergeant pointed to the keys. "Get them," he yelled and in the same instant Colorado scooped them up in his free hand.

"Get me out and we're on our way," O'Hara exulted.

Colorado placed his rifle on the floor and tried different keys while O'Hara, like a mother hen, hovered over him, one hand holding the gun and the other grasping the bar as if he would pull it out by brute strength alone.

Then the lock clicked and the key turned. Anticipation of freedom brought a spark into O'Hara's eyes but it died the instant the rifle boomed out its deathly message. His mouth opened wide and his face contorted as he slumped against the bars. The big hands fought valiantly to retain their grip but, defeated, slid slowly downwards following his body.

Colorado froze and, mesmerised, watched the battle of will. O'Hara looked up at him once before he collapsed on the floor.

Tom Gordon was on his knees and this time levelling the rifle at Colorado's belly, in his own effort of will. Colorado dived at his rifle as the old man's trigger finger flexed. Hitting the floor hard, he grabbed his own rifle and keeping the weapon clear of his body rolled onto his shoulders, and then up, out of the roll, onto one knee. Gordon's bullet missed but the halfbreed poured his outrage into a volley of shots which like successive hammer blows slammed the rancher backward. Jets of blood spurted from the punctures and cascaded onto the cell floor in crimson blurs. Then it was quiet, a funereal silence settling heavily. The two cowboys, feeling death's presence, cowered back, wanting no part of the blood-letting.

Colorado rose woodenly from his knees and stood over O'Hara who lay with one shoulder propped against the bars.

"Get going," O'Hara said in a whisper but the halfbreed bend down beside him and examined the bullet hole. One look told him that O'Hara wouldn't live long and the knowledge showed on his face.

"Get going, damn you," O'Hara repeated, fumbling in the pocket of his tunic. Colorado helped him take the piece of paper out.

"You keep it," the dying man said, crumbling it into the half-breed's hands. "Maybe it'll make up for . . ." The remaining words died with the man in a brief, loud exhalation of breath.

Colorado didn't have time to think. He hurriedly placed the paper in his shirt pocket and leapt to his feet. He paused only to lock the two cowboys in a cell before rushing to the outer office estimating that, since the shots would have been heard, he only had seconds. Once outside in the darkness he would have a chance.

He stepped gingerly onto the broadwalk, cursing the bright moonlight. The clicking of released safety catches stopped him in his tracks and removed hope.

A captain stepped forward and commanded, "Drop your rifle and get back in there."

He thought about fighting it out but the multitude of rifles cancelled any inspiration. He did as he was told, the urge for life still in him.

When they'd taken away the cowboys and the two corpses he was alone again. Curious, he examined the piece of paper O'Hara had slipped him and found it to be a simple sketch map of a stretch of land he knew to be near the Mexican border. O'Hara had marked a cross on it. He put the map away again. Maybe it would be something for the future, maybe not.

26

DEEP in Apache country a tired horseman dismounted, shaded his eyes against the sun's glare, removed his hat and brushed the perspiration from his brow with his shirtsleeve. Gant wasn't a man to give up easily but the quiet monotony of the desert was beginning to get to him and the relentless sun wasn't making it easier. He was a gambler by nature, sometimes by occupation, but he figured this crazy ride was as big a gamble as he'd ever undertaken.

Leaving his horse he sauntered over to a big bunch of cacti. He hacked a piece off with his knife and eagerly held it to his parched, welcoming mouth. As the moisture teased his lips which were demanding more, he tilted his head back and shut his eyes.

Then, temporarily relieved, he replaced

his hat and turned back to his horse. The Apache holding it, standing as still as the desert air, an insolent, mocking look on his face, sent an incongruous shiver through Gant's overheated body. He half-reached for his gun but the Apache's confident impassivity advised caution. Sure enough there was a sudden movement off to the left and Gant saw the reason for his confidence. Three Apaches, coming out of nowhere, had their rifles trained on him as they came forward. Gant's hand fell away from the holster. He knew he was fast but he wasn't that fast.

One of them came right up to him and stood face to face.

"Mimbreno, uh?" Gant asked, hoping.

The mockery in the Apache's eyes descended and spread to the smile which scoffed at Gant from a toothless mouth as he removed the white man's pistol and let it fall.

"Mescalero," he grunted, dropping the smile with the pistol.

Another Apache came closer, his eyes

lighting up with a childish delight when he saw Colorado's necklace around Gant's neck. He gestured at Cant who, reading his meaning, took it off and gave it to him. He put it on and guffawed crazily, pleased with the acquisition. The remaining one of the trio picked up the pistol.

Then they tied his hands with leather thongs and kicked his legs away from him. They didn't bother tying his feet since there was nowhere he could go anyway. After a short huddled debate one of them took a bayonet from a sheath in his belt. The steel glinted in the sun and Gant's stomach muscles tightened as the Apache came towards him. A yard away, he stopped, appraised Gant with a grimacing severity and then, suddenly changing mood, laughed gutturally and made for the white man's horse. With an outburst of manic energy, the Indian gripped the horse's neck, twisted it, dug the bayonet in and ripped. The horse went down fast, kicked its legs in a feeble protest and then died. Gant, forcing himself to watch, so that they would not think him weak, felt sick. He'd had that horse a long time.

The Mescaleros proceeded to build a fire, ignoring him entirely now. Before they lit it, they hacked pieces from the belly of his horse and cut them up. Knowing that Apaches really prized horses, it seemed strange to Gant that they should kill a good horse to feed such a small party.

While they were roasting the meat they came sauntering over, spread-eagled him and staked him out, tying his arms and legs to stakes. One of them piled brushwood over his stomach and it didn't take much intuition for him to work out their intentions. They were going to have two fires: one for cooking horse flesh and one for cooking his innards. He had never known the pure fear that came to him in those moments of realisation.

His captors were tucking into the horse flesh when the other Apaches walked in. Gant counted ten of them and knew why his horse had been killed. This was probably part of a raiding party which had split up. Some of them turned inquisitively in his direction before squatting down and tearing ravenously at the cooked meat. Gant, watching them, sweated with the heat of the sun and dread of what would come. When they'd finished some of them took out clay pipes and smoked, lending a peaceful domesticity to the scene, the antithesis of the barbarism of which he knew they were capable.

Eventually, some of them stood up and took notice of him again. One of them plunged a brand into the fire while the others held their steel knives in the flames.

They came strutting over, like kings of the desert, ready to despatch an interloper. A deluge of sweat burst onto Gant's forehead and ran in rivulets into his eyes, stinging them. They stood over him neither laughing nor particularly serious. The Apache with the flaming brand lowered it casually onto the brushweed and Gant tensed.

He felt the tingling heat on his skin and hoped he would pass out before it reached its maximum.

"Wait!" one of the assembly yelled in Mescalero and kicked away the fire. Gant looked up, confused, and saw the Apache grab Colorado's necklace which hung around the neck of the Mescalero who held the fire-brand.

More words were spoken and the prize was reluctantly removed and handed to the inquisitor who leaned over Gant holding the necklace out.

"Where you get it, white man?" he asked in broken English.

Gant looked around before answering and read curiosity in some of their eyes, disappointment in those of others.

"It's Colorado's," he stated. "Half-breed scout for the soldiers."

"You take it from Colorado?" There was some incredulity in the questioner's voice.

"He is my friend," Gant replied, wondering what this was all about. "Another man stole it. I killed my friend's enemy and took it back."

The Mescalero's eyes narrowed distrustfully. "Where is Colorado?"

"He's in jail at the white man's fort," Gant explained. "I seek the Mimbrenos to tell them of this."

The Apache straightened and indicated that the white man should be untied.

"We are Mescalero," he announced. "But Colorado saved two of us near the big river. We owe him two lives!"

He studied Gant more closely.

"We will take you to the Mimbreno. Magnas Colorado will decide if your words are straight."

27

COLORADO watched the red glow spreading like fire in the eastern sky as the sun rose and called forth all life. The solitary bugle played a plaintive reveille as two troopers ran the flag up in man's ceremonial announcement of another day. Watching and listening was given extra poignancy for Colorado, since this was the end of it all; today he was seeing his last dawn.

He lay down again on the bed and stared vacantly at the ceiling, with little fear. He wasn't too concerned about his imminent death. His main concern, as he lay there, was for his mother, for Brannigan and Diego. He wouldn't be around to protect them if trouble should come their way and, more than that, he feared his mother would take his death badly, blaming herself for leaving the Mimbrenos.

When his escort came, he was still calm and collected, stretching himself proudly to his full height, towering over the soldiers. Outside the sun had reached its full glory and seemed a live and curious witness to the coming negation of his life. A light breeze from the desert drifted in and wafted the flag as he was marched on to the parade ground to face the assembled firing squad.

General Crook and his officers, imperious-looking on their horses, were watching the proceedings. As he looked into the eyes of the firing squad Colorado felt degraded. The Apache in him protested against this death; it was not a man's death to be led this way like a meek lamb to the slaughter. But fate had decreed this and for him there could be no honourable death now.

He braced himself as Crook prodded his horse forward to come level with the firing squad.

"Shoulder arms," the General's voice

boomed out and twelve rifles came up simultaneously like twelve parts of a precision machine, independent, but working for a common end. But before they could bring about that end two of the rifles fell to the ground followed by two bodies emitting pained screams. The blue line parted in confusion. Two Apache war lances, older purveyors of death than the rifles but sometimes equally effective, protruded between the shoulder blades of the writhing soldiers.

General Crook's horse shied and kicked nervously as the line broke completely and the men ran for cover. But ten arrows, whistling and sighing their lamentations, chased their appointed targets and cut them down.

The officers' horses bucked and whinnied as they sensed death and danger. Colorado scanned the roofs of the flat adobe buildings and saw them come to life as the Mimbrenos rose from their hiding places, leapt to the ground and swarmed all over the fort. But their movements were not haphazard. Well trained guerilla fighters, they moved in groups, one group to each of the fort's main buildings; Colorado saw Magnas's hand in it all. It took only seconds to surround the key buildings. Crook and the officers, struggling to control their mounts, had only half drawn their hand guns when they were encircled by Mimbrenos whose arrows were pointed menacingly. The half-dressed troops, dashing from their quarters, met the same sight and halted abruptly, staring helplessly at these infiltrators who had stolen in by night. Every man was soon accounted for and an expectant silence settled. Mimbreno fingers tensed on their bow strings while icy fingers of apprehension gripped the white men's stomachs.

All eyes followed Magnas Colorado as he walked proudly towards his nephew. In his hands now lay the power of life and death.

"Today, nephew, you have looked death in the eye and cheated it,"

Magnas pronounced, looking around the fort.

Colorado grasped his uncle's hand, his affection and gratitude mingling. "How did you know, wise one?"

"Your friend, the one called Gant."

Colorado smiled to himself, remembering how Gant had told him that one day he might need him. That had certainly proved true.

"Where is Gant, uncle?"

"Mexico. He told me, if this went right, he would maybe see you in Sonora."

"Thanks to you that may be," Colorado replied, looking round the fort. "But what will you do with the bluecoats?" He was afraid of the reply. His uncle's hatred of the white men was well documented in blood.

Magnas grunted. "I promised Gant I would kill only as necessary. It is worth your life. But I will strip the fort bare."

Colorado was relieved at those words. "I thank my uncle a thousand times."

Magnas' eyes smiled. "What will you do now that this is over?"

"I will go to Mexico, and maybe find Gant."

Magnas did not argue. He did not need to tell his nephew he would be welcome to live with the Mimbreno any time. He called for a horse and one of his men brought a black stallion forward, saying in Apache tongue that it was the best of the horses in the stable.

"No bluecoat will catch you on that horse," Magnas said.

Colorado took the halter, mounted and glanced round the fort.

"We will not kill them," Magnas repeated. "But we will take away everything we can carry. Winter will be long in the mountains."

"We will meet again," Colorado said, turning the horse's head.

"In a better world than this perhaps." Magnas replied, thinking his own son would be of age with Colorado if the whites had not killed him.

He turned away as Colorado rode off. There was work to be done now.

As he rode, Colorado thought how easy the rescue had been. That morning death had seemed certain. Now he had another chance.

28

CONSIDERING he was a big man, O'Hara's hand had been delicate and precise when he had drawn up his map. Colorado had no difficulty finding the spot he had marked and had to admit to himself that he was real curious about what lay buried there. Purposely had ridden this way on the route to Mexico; it had only involved a small deviation from his intended journey.

He tethered his horse near some galleto grass and headed towards the big pinon tree, scouring the surrounding area for something he could use as a digging implement. He decided a sharp stone would do but, if whatever lay there was really deep down, he'd have to find an alternative.

He lifted the pile of rocks on the south side of the tree, took a big breath and started scraping. The soil was loose enough and would have been easily movable with a spade, but was much more difficult with the stone. In a half hour he was a foot down and despairing a little, when suddenly there was a dark piece of leather protruding and he dug at it harder until the shape of a saddlebag became distinct. He tugged at it with his hands and it resisted, stubbornly, like an ancient secret. So he dug deeper and tried again. This time the saddlebag came away and he fell backwards.

He undid the straps and turned the bag upside down. The bundles of notes came pouring out like released prisoners and they piled up, one upon another. He sat cross-legged, Buddha-like on the ground, and stared at the money but he was not, as some would have done, worshipping it. He was mainly surprised.

Picking up a bundle he thumbed through it, counting the notes. Next he counted the bundles and estimated the total. He figured that there was at least enough to keep him for three years on easy street, not a king's ransom but enough for a lone half-breed in need of a stake.

He bundled the money into the saddlebag, went back to his horse and climbed up. For a few minutes he sat motionless, thinking of the strip of blue water which was the Rio Grande. On the other side was Mexico, his destination. But he knew there was something he had to do now before he could cross that river. Previously, when he was escaping, it had been the rescue of the Mimbreno slaves which had delayed him and given Tidy his chance. This time it was a vision in his own mind which held him back; the vision of a beautiful yellow-haired girl dying in his arms and her sad pleas for her son's future welfare. It came back to him from the past insistently and, knowing what he had to do, he spurred the black stallion. It would be a long ride there and back and night was encroaching now.

★ ★ ★

That next morning Brannigan rose early, as usual, stretched, wiped the sleep from his eyes and strode onto the wooden porch in his nightshirt. He raised his eyes upwards, studying the sky, and then moved forward heading for the water barrel. The curse he let out as one of his bare feet tripped against something was lost in the vast open spaces surrounding. When he had finished hopping around on one leg, he turned and saw the offending saddlebag lying on the wooden board. Warily he walked back, studied it and then picked it up. The note inside fluttered to the ground. Brannigan picked it up and read: 'For Diego.'

On a ridge above the cabin Colorado smiled and turned his horse southwards again. This time he would make it.

Other titles in the Linford Western Library:

TOP HAND
Wade Everett

The Broken T was big. But no ranch is big enough to let a man hide from himself.

GUN WOLVES OF LOBO BASIN
Lee Floren

The Feud was a blood debt. When Smoke Talbot found the outlaws who gunned down his folks he aimed to nail their hide to the barn door.

SHOTGUN SHARKEY
Marshall Grover

The westbound coach carrying the indomitable Larry and Stretch headed for a shooting showdown.

FIGHTING RAMROD
Charles N. Heckelmann

Most men would have cut their losses, but Frazer counted the bullets in his guns and said he'd soak the range in blood before he'd give up another inch of what was his.

LONE GUN
Eric Allen

Smoke Blackbird had been away too long. The Lequires had seized the Blackbird farm, forcing the Indians and settlers off, and no one seemed willing to fight! He had to fight alone.

THE THIRD RIDER
Barry Cord

Mel Rawlins wasn't going to let anything stand in his way. His father was murdered, his two brothers gone. Now Mel rode for vengeance.

ARIZONA DRIFTERS
W. C. Tuttle

When drifting Dutton and Lonnie Steelman decide to become partners they find that they have a common enemy in the formidable Thurston brothers.

TOMBSTONE
Matt Braun

Wells Fargo paid Luke Starbuck to outgun the silver-thieving stagecoach gang at Tombstone. Before long Luke can see the only thing bearing fruit in this eldorado will be the gallows tree.

HIGH BORDER RIDERS
Lee Floren

Buckshot McKee and Tortilla Joe cut the trail of a border tough who was running Mexican beef into Texas. They stopped the smuggler in his tracks.

BRETT RANDALL, GAMBLER
E. B. Mann

Larry Day had the choice of running away from the law or of assuming a dead man's place. No matter what he decided he was bound to end up dead.

THE GUNSHARP
William R. Cox

The Eggerleys weren't very smart. They trained their sights on Will Carney and Arizona's biggest blood bath began.

THE DEPUTY OF SAN RIANO
Lawrence A. Keating and
Al. P. Nelson

When a man fell dead from his horse, Ed Grant was spotted riding away from the scene. The deputy sheriff rode out after him and came up against everything from gunfire to dynamite.

FARGO: MASSACRE RIVER
John Benteen

The ambushers up ahead had now blocked the road. Fargo's convoy was a jumble, a perfect target for the insurgents' weapons!

SUNDANCE: DEATH IN THE LAVA
John Benteen

The Modoc's captured the wagon train and its cargo of gold. But now the halfbreed they called Sundance was going after it ...

HARSH RECKONING
Phil Ketchum

Five years of keeping himself alive in a brutal prison had made Brand tough and careless about who he gunned down ...

FARGO: PANAMA GOLD
John Benteen

With foreign money behind him, Buckner was going to destroy the Panama Canal before it could be completed. Fargo's job was to stop Buckner.

FARGO: THE SHARPSHOOTERS
John Benteen

The Canfield clan, thirty strong were raising hell in Texas. Fargo was tough enough to hold his own against the whole clan.

PISTOL LAW
Paul Evan Lehman

Lance Jones came back to Mustang for just one thing — revenge! Revenge on the people who had him thrown in jail.

HELL RIDERS
Steve Mensing

Wade Walker's kid brother, Duane, was locked up in the Silver City jail facing a rope at dawn. Wade was a ruthless outlaw, but he was smart, and he had vowed to have his brother out of jail before morning!

DESERT OF THE DAMNED
Nelson Nye

The law was after him for the murder of a marshal — a murder he didn't commit. Breen was after him for revenge — and Breen wouldn't stop at anything . . . blackmail, a frameup . . . or murder.

DAY OF THE COMANCHEROS
Steven C. Lawrence

Their very name struck terror into men's hearts — the Comancheros, a savage army of cutthroats who swept across Texas, leaving behind a bloodstained trail of robbery and murder.

SUNDANCE: SILENT ENEMY
John Benteen

A lone crazed Cheyenne was on a personal war path. They needed to pit one man against one crazed Indian. That man was Sundance.

LASSITER
Jack Slade

Lassiter wasn't the kind of man to listen to reason. Cross him once and he'll hold a grudge for years to come — if he let you live that long.

LAST STAGE TO GOMORRAH
Barry Cord

Jeff Carter, tough ex-riverboat gambler, now had himself a horse ranch that kept him free from gunfights and card games. Until Sturvesant of Wells Fargo showed up.

McALLISTER ON THE COMANCHE CROSSING
Matt Chisholm

The Comanche, McAllister owes them a life — and the trail is soaked with the blood of the men who had tried to outrun them before.

QUICK-TRIGGER COUNTRY
Clem Colt

Turkey Red hooked up with Curly Bill Graham's outlaw crew. But wholesale murder was out of Turk's line, so when range war flared he bucked the whole border gang alone . . .

CAMPAIGNING
Jim Miller

Ambushed on the Santa Fe trail, Sean Callahan is saved by two Indian strangers. But there'll be more lead and arrows flying before the band join Kit Carson against the Comanches.

GUNSLINGER'S RANGE
Jackson Cole

Three escaped convicts are out for revenge. They won't rest until they put a bullet through the head of the dirty snake who locked them behind bars.

RUSTLER'S TRAIL
Lee Floren

Jim Carlin knew he would have to stand up and fight because he had staked his claim right in the middle of Big Ike Outland's best grass.

THE TRUTH ABOUT SNAKE RIDGE
Marshall Grover

The troubleshooters came to San Cristobal to help the needy. For Larry and Stretch the turmoil began with a brawl and then an ambush.

WOLF DOG RANGE
Lee Floren

Will Ardery would stop at nothing, unless something stopped him first — like a bullet from Pete Manly's gun.

DEVIL'S DINERO
Marshall Grover

Plagued by remorse, a rich old reprobate hired the Texas Troubleshooters to deliver a fortune in greenbacks to each of his victims.

GUNS OF FURY
Ernest Haycox

Dane Starr, alias Dan Smith, wanted to close the door on his past and hang up his guns, but people wouldn't let him.